Praise for George... s
A Wine... e

There is nothing better than a riveting story about titanic battles between the forces of good and evil. Throw in some social commentary, historic reflections, struggles of faith and conscience, a Brave New World of science gone mad, and a dash of romance. The result is a truer-than-fiction peek into a frightening future that is headed our way—unless we take a stand with the forces of good.

Without being preachy, the author warns that rejecting godly values could lead an ethically challenged society to create soulless, robotic killers like those in his book. That is why we need heroes like Drake, who "believes in good and evil, that wrong should be righted, and that justice should be done."
—*HIGHLANDS TODAY* (Sebring, Fla.)

This is a very good science fiction thriller that entertains and challenges at the same time. As described by Duncan, the future seems, if not inevitable, at least plausible—at times fascinating and at times chilling. But he also offers hope.
—*ASHLAND* (Ore.) *DAILY TIDINGS*

Give human beings 6,000 years after the fall in Eden and what will they create?

"Something evil," a red-haired beauty tells Jerico Drake, the hero of *A Wine Red Silence,* a fast-paced novel. In it, Drake, a "genplus" (genetically enhanced) private investigator, takes on humans with a robot's conscience and robots with a human's cunning...(the novel) catapults current ethical concerns into a hard-edged, hard-wired world.
—*HUNTSVILLE TIMES*

Novels by George L. Duncan

A Cold and Distant Memory
A Wine Red Silence
A Dark Orange Farewell
Galaxy Gems

A DARK ORANGE FAREWELL

A DARK ORANGE FAREWELL

GEORGE L. DUNCAN

OakTara

WATERFORD, VIRGINIA

A Dark Orange Farewell

Published in the U.S. by:
OakTara Publishers
P.O. Box 8
Waterford, VA 20197

Visit OakTara at
www.oaktara.com

Cover design by David LaPlaca/debest design co.
Cover images © iStockphoto.com/Tom Werner, Nick Tzolov, Soren Pilman

ISBN: 978-1-60290-113-1

A Dark Orange Farewell is a work of fiction. References to real people, events, establishments, organizations, or locales are intended only to provide a sense of authenticity and are used fictitiously. All other characters, incidents, and dialogue are drawn from the author's imagination.

To Michelle,
a courageous light
fighting back the darkness.

To Becca,
thanks for
the copyreading.

To Kathleen,
who is adorable.

One

There was light early morning traffic on Savannah Avenue, but in this section of the city I doubted there was ever heavy traffic. The sun came up glaring between the bumps that people in Florida call hills. For a minute or two, before the day burned with the regular Sunshine State ferocity, the sky reflected the deep blue of creation,

I drove slowly through Quail Ridge, past the tennis courts and swimming pools and the two-story houses that were just a couple of rooms shy of being mansions. With the rapid expansion of the economy, I wasn't sure if the houses were a display of new wealth or old wealth. I half expected an iron gate with a guard at the entrance, but the house I was looking for merely had a wide driveway leading to a contemporary residence spread out over a slope. The slope ran steeply down to the edge of a golf course where dew glistened on the green fairway. White pillars contrasted with the yellow trim on the house. Over the door was a ceramic circle that looked like the head of a lion.

I wondered if a butler would greet me, but Bolly Canterley opened the door before I knocked. He was a handsome, stocky man with curly brown hair, green eyes, but a haggard look. He hadn't shaved, and the beard stubble stuck out like jagged cactus spines.

"Come in," he said.

I walked into a large living room decked in green. A woman wearing a pale yellow bathrobe that didn't match the decor stood at a doorway. She had her arms crossed with a cigarette stuck between two fingers of her left hand. She showed me a wan smile. There was something that bothered me about her posture, but I couldn't define it.

Canterley gestured toward me. "Geneva, this is Jarrod Banyon, the private detective I called."

As acknowledgement, she brought the cigarette to her lips, inhaled, and blew out some smoke.

"Let's go into my study," he said.

I followed him, and his wife followed me. Canterley walked down a hall and into a room filled with paintings and bookshelves. He slid behind a large, oak desk and sat in a black office chair. His wife perched on the edge of the desk.

"I gather there's been no word from your daughter."

He shook his head. "No. And, as I mentioned, there are two guns missing from the house."

"Bolly is a member of a hunt club. Members go out a couple of times a year," Geneva said. She puffed on her cigarette, then snubbed it out in an orange seashell ashtray. "We have dozens of guns around."

"Only twelve handguns, Mr. Banyon," he said quickly, almost apologetically. "I'm a collector—"

"Bullets?"

"Yes." There was a pause. "Four cases of cartridges are also missing."

"Do you know why she would take a gun, or guns?"

He shook his head.

"Stephanie has gone shooting with her father occasionally, on ranges. She doesn't like hunting," Geneva said. "She has some athletic ability and is an excellent shot but, unlike her father, she's never been fascinated with guns."

Maybe she is now, I thought.

She brought out a cigarette pack from a pocket in her housecoat and slapped the pack against her hand until a cigarette popped out. She fashioned her lips around the filter, then flicked a lighter. Whereas her husband seemed edgy, her movements suggested defiance, as if telling the world it wasn't her fault that her daughter was missing.

"When was the last time you saw Stephanie?" I asked.

She pushed up the sleeve of the robe and checked her watch. "About twenty-three hours ago. She left for her high school yesterday, and I haven't seen her since."

"She drove?"

"Yes," Canterley said. "Stephanie has her own car."

"Credit cards?"

"No. She has her own bank account, though. I believe several thousand dollars are in it." He glanced toward his wife again.

"Do you have any idea why Stephanie would run away?"

His wife answered. "No. We had a disagreement yesterday, but it was no reason for her to take off. She yelled at my husband and me and told us our fortune was built on theft and lies."

"Any reason for such an outburst?"

At first there was no response. The question bobbed in the air like a buoy in the ocean, refusing to be swept away by time or tides.

"She's become a religious crazy," Geneva said.

Canterley didn't seem to disagree with his wife's assessment. He turned toward me. "Three months ago Stephanie became what is known as a born-again Christian."

I showed a gentle smile. "Well, at least she didn't spike her hair, take dope, and get tattoos."

"Perhaps that would have been better," Geneva said. She lifted back her head to blow the smoke toward the ceiling. "Ever deal with born-again Christians, Mr. Banyon?"

"No, but I hear some of them are quite nice. My job is usually with once-born people, and some of them are rather nasty."

3

"Some born-agains may be nice but our daughter became insufferable. She questioned aspects of our life, our background, our fortune...it was that boyfriend of hers that started it."

"She has a boyfriend?"

"A boy named Ted Landers. He's older than she is."

"Not by much," Canterley said. "Ted is twenty-one. In a month Stephanie will be eighteen. Ted is the one who took her to Souls Harbor. It's a church about ten miles from here. He's born-again, and he infected Stephanie."

"I think Christians prefer the term *converted*," I said.

"I don't care what they prefer. I didn't raise my daughter to be a Bible-thumper. Besides, aren't Christians against stealing?" Geneva said.

"Maybe she didn't consider taking the guns as stealing. They were in the house, and she used them so—"

"Taking the figurine was stealing. There's no other word for it."

I gave her a blank stare.

It was her husband who answered. "Late last night, when Stephanie didn't return home, I phoned her best friend, Tiffany Danielson. She informed me Stephanie had been over there yesterday afternoon. Tiffany's parents own Sea Island Galleries. They deal in antiques. At their house they had an antique figurine, a small replica of an Aztec god. Shortly after Stephanie left, they discovered it was missing."

"Why would she take that? Is it worth much?"

Canterley sighed. "It's not easily disposed of, but I think, with the proper contacts, it could be sold for anywhere from five to ten thousand dollars."

"But if she wanted to sell it, wouldn't the buyer of an item like that ask questions?"

He nodded. "That type of money could probably be obtained only through legitimate buyers and shops."

"But you said she probably has several thousand in her bank

account."

"Yes. I have no idea why she took the figurine, if she did."

There was something odd about the atmosphere in the room. For some reason I remembered a camping trip made years ago with a friend. We were hiking with several others and stopped to rest. As we sat down on the ground I was uneasy. I kept looking around. The wariness grew, but it was not until we stood up to leave that I spotted the reason for my anxiety. A diamondback had curled up behind a bush. The head slid up and down, and the tongue flicked out of its mouth. For some reason, the tail stayed still. There was no rattle of danger. I wondered if I should check behind Canterley's desk for snakes.

"Where is the gun case?"

"I'll show you."

I followed Canterley as he walked to an adjoining room where bookshelves reached to the ceiling. Two obscure paintings hung on the walls. Vivid hues of orange and black sketched an abstract landscape with vague sharp symbols in the background. Although I didn't like his taste in art, Canterley was much neater than me. The gun cabinet was spotless. The ten remaining weapons in the gun case were polished and shining. An empty, dustfree slot appeared in the top row. Below it and to the left another space was empty. A taller, more rectangular cabinet held rifles, but all of the longer guns were in their proper places.

"What type of guns were taken?" I asked.

"A Kimber Desert Warrior pistol and a Fobus GLC."

For a gun enthusiast, he didn't seem to know the significance of the choices. I opened the case, took a brief look, then closed it. We walked back to the study, where he sat down behind his desk again.

"Before the argument yesterday, were there any indications she might take off?"

Both hesitated before answering. "There were normal

tensions between parents and a teenager. Nothing more," Canterley said.

"Normal tensions don't usually result in a girl taking two guns and running away."

He didn't answer but slipped his hand inside the desk and brought out a blue checkbook. He flopped it on the desk blotter. "As I told Geneva, Ben Murdock is a business associate, and he's the one who mentioned your name to me, Mr. Banyon. I understand you handled a delicate matter for him several years ago."

I nodded.

"He told me it was handled discreetly and very efficiently." I added a smile to the nod.

"We would require the same type of professionalism."

"Of course," I said.

I realized I didn't have great affection for either Bolly or Geneva Canterley, but that's an emotion unnecessary for private detectives. I also wasn't sure I trusted them, which was more bothersome.

"Dealing with once-born rich people, I ask for money up front," I said.

Canterley's cactus stubble bristled with indignation. "You're rather insolent, Mr. Banyon."

"Didn't Ben Murdock tell you that too?"

He leaned back in the chair. He arched his eyebrows and gave a low hiss. Then he shrugged. "We're not paying you for your manners." He flipped open the checkbook, scribbled quickly with a pen, ripped a check off, and handed it to me. "It's for five thousand dollars. Will that be sufficient?"

I nodded and took the check. "Do you think Stephanie ran away with Ted? Have you phoned him?"

"I assume that, but we don't have a phone number or address for Ted."

I thought that was odd, but said nothing.

"Mr. Banyon, our daughter stole a valuable artifact from people who have been friends of ours for twenty years. It must be returned." His statement held particular vehemence.

"I'll see what I can do."

"You will keep us informed?" Canterley's tone was halfway between a plea and a warning.

"Yes. Do you have a picture?"

"Of the figurine? No. But the Danielsons would."

I'm not an emotional, touchy-feely kind of guy. Even so, I was a bit shocked by his response.

"Do you have a picture of Stephanie?" I asked in a strictly professional tone.

"I'll get you one," Geneva said.

I started to walk out. Canterley followed me. "We've been through a shock, Mr. Banyon, and we didn't sleep last night. Forgive us if we haven't made a good first impression."

"Forget about it," I said.

Geneva came back and handed me a three-by-five color shot of her daughter. After talking with her parents, I was surprised at the kindness and vitality reflected in Stephanie's eyes. She was a light blond with alert blue eyes and a golden smile.

"That was taken about a year ago," her mother said.

"How is she doing in school? Any signs of trouble?"

She shook her head. "Our daughter has always been an exceptional student. She's taking advanced placement classes. Her GPA is above four."

I took the photograph and placed it in my inside coat pocket.

Geneva, another cigarette stuck in her mouth, stared at me. "By the way, do you carry a weapon?" she asked.

I lifted my coat to let her see the Glock.

"You carry a big gun."

"Had to shoot some big people."

I should never try humor before nine a.m. Mornings are not my best time.

Geneva didn't smile. "Do all private detectives have your rather mordant sense of humor, Mr. Banyon?"

"No, they don't." I smiled. "I'm unique."

She took a deep puff on her cigarette, then pulled it out of her mouth. As she exhaled smoke, her eyes looked beyond me. "Perhaps too much so," she said, but I wasn't sure who the words were directed at.

As I went down the front steps I turned back and glanced at the house. I realized the ceramic lion wasn't a lion at all. It was a human face on the circle, some god of mythology, a malignant and angry deity of a long-forgotten people.

Two

The Danielson house was slightly bigger but just as uninviting as the house I'd just left. This one was perched on a small hill. The windows, surrounded by red shutters, looked like eyes that stared warily across the countryside looking for prey. A light morning fog crept along the road. A yellow school bus came toward me. As it passed I heard the giggles and shouts of children, but the sounds seemed out of place.

The house had no ceramic deity but a large, gold knocker on the double front door. Canterley said he would call ahead so they would be expecting me. When I clanged once, the door was opened by a blond woman in a blue business suit. She looked alert and irritated.

"Mr. Banyon?"

"Yes."

"I'm Carmen Danielson. Please come in."

I walked into a hall and down the corridor to a large living room decorated in silver. The fireplace was enclosed, next to the huge flat-screen television.

The woman sighed. "I can't tell you how much this has upset us."

"It upset the Canterleys too."

Mrs. Danielson paced back and forth like a drill sergeant. "Our daughter was friends with Stephanie. We'd never dreamed she'd do anything like this. And to steal our artifact."

"Can you think of any reason why she'd do that?"

She shook her head. A bookcase was next to the television. I skimmed the titles but didn't see anything familiar. The Danielsons had rather esoteric tastes. The bookcase ended at a doorway. The last book on the second row, *Ancient Altars,* stuck out about two inches. I pushed it back into line.

Shouts came from beyond the doorway. A slender brunette with startling gray eyes backed into the room. As she edged passed me, an angry barrel of a man stepped toward her. The ugly shade of red in his face seemed to glow deeper as he walked.

"I did not know she took it, Dad, if she did."

"If?" he yelled. "There's no if about it. Why was she over here yesterday?"

"She just came over. We talked briefly and she left. We never went close to your office."

He brought back his hand. "If you're lying to me, you little—"

"Gary!"

He swung, but I caught his wrist and twisted his arm. My fingers bit into his skin. He groaned and dropped down to one knee.

"Maybe you should calm down," I told him.

I gave his arm one final jerk. It threw him off balance. He slapped his other hand on the silver carpet to keep from falling.

I looked over at Tiffany. She had not flinched when threatened. She stood defiant, the gray eyes flowing with anger and sadness.

Danielson pushed himself up. "Who are you?"

"Jarrod Banyon."

"The private detective?"

"One and the same."

He snorted, but I wasn't sure if it was from pain or derision. "Then maybe you should question my daughter. Maybe you can get more information than I can."

"I'll use different methods too."

10

Carmen walked over and became a blue barrier before her red-faced husband and her gray-eyed daughter. "Tiffany, why don't you leave us alone for a moment."

"Make it a day or a week. Or a lifetime," she said as she strode out of the room, but the voice wasn't as hostile as the words. When she disappeared, Carmen turned to me. "You have to understand, this is a very difficult period for us."

"He doesn't have to understand anything," her husband said in a voice full of anger and pain. "He gets paid to do a job. We want the job done, not his understanding."

Danielson held his arm, groaned, and walked around to a couch where he plopped down. He looked at me, from head to feet. "There's a military bearing about you. Been in the service?"

"Yes."

"Seen combat?"

I didn't like his questions. "Yes. Want to know if I killed anyone?" When he didn't respond, I said, "And you're not paying me for any job."

"The Canterleys are, and if you're not successful, they'll be paying us big time. I'll sue them for the cost of—"

"Please sit down, Mr. Banyon," Carmen said.

I eased down into a chair while Carmen went to a portable bar and fixed a drink. She handed it to her husband. "It's early, but today we can use one." He took it, saying nothing.

When she had fixed a second and sipped it, she turned back to me. "I don't usually explain family matters to strangers, Mr. Banyon, but today I feel I should. The theft of that artifact has put us in a very, very difficult position. It could not have come at a worse time. I assure you my husband doesn't hit our daughter. Tiffany, from time to time, suffers from depression. Usually we are very solicitous of her."

She paused and sat down next to her husband. She leaned forward, putting her elbows on her knees. She rolled the glass between her hands. "Recently we have experienced a series of financial reversals. Dealing with antiques is precarious. You're always on the financial edge. The overhead is tremendous, and usually you don't know if anyone will buy the item that you've just purchased for thousands of dollars."

She sipped from the glass and then resumed her position. Her hands were so deft, the liquid rarely moved as she turned the glass. "We are, frankly, in rather desperate need for some immediate cash. A buyer has promised to buy this particular artifact for fifty thousand dollars."

"But I was told it was only worth about ten thousand at most."

"Whoever said that didn't know the true value of the item. At auction, it could probably bring at least thirty-five thousand. We have a customer who is an ardent collector and is passionate about Aztec artifacts. This is the piece he wanted, and he was willing to pay for it. It was time-consuming for us to obtain, but the effort was about to pay off. We're not just looking at the loss of one item, it could be the loss of our business."

"I'll get it back for you."

"Thank you. I hope you can."

"You have a picture of it?"

She nodded.

Her husband stood. "I'll get one for you," he said.

She tapped herself on her forehead. "Oh, I'm sorry, Mr. Banyon. I didn't offer you a drink. Unlike us, I didn't think you needed one, but would you like a cup of coffee perhaps?"

"Coffee would be nice."

She set down her glass and walked toward the back of the house. I wanted to be alone for a minute. There were no snakes in the Danielsons' living room, but I felt a vague sense of unease. Something about her story just didn't resonate. I didn't see why she would lie, but I sensed Carmen Danielson could make a polygraph beep just by looking at it.

She walked back into the room and handed me a blue cup

and saucer. I thanked her and sipped the coffee.

A minute later her husband came back in and showed me a snapshot of the artifact. It was an ugly little thing. Squat and black, with gold and red markings. The male figure had its jaws open in a hideous grin. Or perhaps a scream. In one hand it held a sacrificial knife. If I were a superstitious type, it would have sent chills down my spine.

My mind was so focused on the figure, I didn't catch Gary Danielson's first sentences.

"...it is five, maybe six hundred years old, the finest example of art of that period—"

"I'm not sure I'd call this art," I said.

"It may be different than what you usually see, but that doesn't mean the culture that made it was inferior, nor does it make the figure any less valuable."

I stared at the picture again and decided I didn't want to live in a society that produced this creature.

"Didn't the Aztecs practice human sacrifice?"

"Yes, at times they could be a savage race, but they also had many admirable traits."

"I doubt the guys on the altar felt so."

I eased the picture inside my coat pocket, right next to the photograph of Stephanie Canterley. The beauty and the beast. I asked Danielson to show me where he kept the figure, then followed as he led me through the house.

In the back, on a table half the size of a football field, about a dozen figures lay on cloths, as if waiting to be polished for buyers. Not all were as squat and ugly as the Aztec figure. A few were taller. Two or three were graphically male or female. Minor gods of a blood-drenched altar. Their value had increased with the passing of centuries. Not, I thought, an example of progress. On the far wall, two dark African masks stared down at the figures.

Danielson walked to a spot on the table where blue cloths

were spread. By the indentation, a heavy object had set there once.

"Right there," he said.

"Did Stephanie Canterley ever come in here?"

"Not to my knowledge. She has never shown any interest in antiques, at least not to me."

I looked at the other figures. "Why take just one? Why not take all of them?"

"For one thing, they're heavy. One figure would weigh about twenty-five or thirty pounds. It would be difficult to haul them all off."

"Why pick that one?"

Danielson just shook his head.

"I'd like to talk to Tiffany."

Carmen Danielson glanced at her watch. "When Bolly Canterley told us he hired you, we thought you might, so I haven't taken her to school yet. We're buying Tiffany a new car, but it won't be ready until tomorrow. We sold her last one."

"I can take her. It will give us a chance to talk."

Her husband still wore an angry scowl. I could almost hear him growling. He moved his shoulder while shifting his weight from one foot to the other, like an angry bull pawing the ground. Looking at the couple, the thought came to me that Tiffany must be adopted. She bore absolutely no resemblance to her father and none that I could see to her mother. Definitely an odd couple. Maybe that's what working around odious little figures does to you.

Tiffany Danielson didn't speak as she walked to my car. She was surprised when I opened the door for her and responded with a quick smile. I got in the driver's side and followed her directions.

For several blocks she was silent, then turned to me.

"I should thank you, Mr. Banyon, for stopping my father from hitting me."

"Does he do that often?"

"No...his behavior..." She looked out the window.

I turned left at her request.

"It's not really his fault," she said. "I think his antiques are creepy, but he lives for them. He loves the past. I just happen to be in his present."

"Sometimes if you get caught up in the past, it can destroy the future."

She wore a rueful smile. "Maybe that's what my parents are afraid of—that the future will catch up with them."

I made another turn when she directed. I studied the young woman. There was no current sign of depression. The gray eyes reflected intelligence. Her short brown hair was expertly shaped to heighten her attractive tan face.

"I'm on your side, Tiffany."

She turned a questioning gaze toward me. "And Stephanie and Ted? Are you on their side too?"

"Yes. I've met Stephanie's parents."

That prompted a quick laugh. Then her look became solemn again. "But you would take her back to them?"

"Not if she doesn't want to go."

There was another silence while we stopped at a red light. Her alert eyes held me in their gaze.

"They may need a friend," I told her. "Do you know why they fled?"

Her eyes softened, and the gaze turned friendly. "That I don't know, and it's shocking. Steph is not one to be unpredictable or to do rash things."

"Can you tell me something about her?"

She smiled. "There's any number of positive adjectives to use about Stephanie. She's extremely bright, gets straight A's, is friendly and caring. She volunteers at the local retirement center. That tells you something about her." She gestured, making a broad sweep with her hand. "Look around you, Mr. Banyon. Most people here are not hurting for money, and their kids often reflect the narcissism of the rich. Life is all about them. They're callous and selfish. Stephanie wasn't like that."

"Proving there are limits to genetics."

She laughed again. "I never could figure out her parents either. Stephanie became a Christian a few months ago. I witnessed to her because it seemed like a natural fit. She'd be attracted to a God of love who wants to help people. Her parents were upset when they heard the news. If she had told them she was sleeping with her boyfriend, they'd shrug and say fine."

"Tell me about the boyfriend. Could he have influenced Stephanie?"

She shook her head. "Ted has a good mind too, but...I don't think this was his idea. I think Stephanie has the stronger, more assertive personality...not that Ted is a doormat, but he generally goes along with her. He's much better than Chad."

I looked at her. "Who is Chad?"

"Chad Atkinson. I don't want to say he was Stephanie's boyfriend before Ted. I don't think she was that close to him, but they did hang out a little. Played a little tennis together. Had an occasional lunch. He..."

"He what?"

"Chad...to be frank, Mr. Banyon, I don't know. He seemed to be nice enough, but I just never warmed to him. He never did anything to send alarms off. I just never enjoyed being in his company."

"Is he a student too?"

"No, he's older. I think he's twenty-two and has a degree. He's an assistant pharmacist at one of the regional drug stores here. But he's been out of Stephanie's life for about two, three months, not that he was ever really in it."

16

She looked at me, this time with some wariness. "What worries me is that Stephanie is pretty emotionally centered. She rolls with the punches and flows with the tide. She doesn't let events upset her. Besides, she's been accepted by three universities, including Florida Atlantic, where Ted is. Taking off doesn't make sense." She paused for a minute. Her gaze looked toward the horizon, then shifted back to me. "The thing is, Stephanie doesn't do anything without a reason."

"You think she took the artifact?"

I pulled into the school parking lot. Tiffany sighed before answering. "I can't imagine why. She was over the day it was found missing, and she was interested in it. She had asked some questions about it, but there was no reason for her to steal it."

There was concern on her face, but her smile was so bright I asked about the depression.

"On and off for some years," she told me. "It's been heavy for about a week—I went back on my medication for a while—but when I woke up this morning it had lifted. It's like being in the middle of a dense fog, if that fog has black hands squeezing your skull. This morning, the sunshine broke through."

Her hand grabbed the door handle. She opened it, swung her legs out, then bent back inside. "Stephanie and Ted are good together. I told them they reminded me of Romeo and Juliet. But now I remember that play was a tragedy."

"Yes. Both characters died. As did a number of other people."

"You didn't lie to me, did you, Mr. Banyon? You will help them?"

"I will. I promise."

She smiled and closed the door.

As I drove out of the parking lot, I noticed the swirling, black clouds in the distance. A storm was speeding our way. Two bolts of lightning flared briefly, then vanished in the blackness.

The dawn had reflected the innocent blue of Creation, but time had moved on. It was now after the Fall.

Three

The drive to Souls Harbor took me north into Flagler County, an area of the Sunshine State that still has scenic and rural patches between the four-lane highways and malls. But the voracious Blight Monster, not content with the decayed remains of cities and sites in the southern part of the state, always seeks new land to despoil. It hovers around fresh acreage to transform beauty into ugliness. It's not one huge beast, but hundreds of vicious, small ones, much like the ghastly figures of the Danielsons. Encroaching from both coasts, they have digested citrus groves, pastures, scenic trails, and trampled deer and opossum while spitting out beer cans, plastic cartons, fast-food lunch boxes, and other assorted debris. There are still random bits of beauty, but the monsters loom, always greedy and hungry, waiting for a chance to destroy.

The Aztec idols and the sprawl gods always demand new sacrifices to devour. They are never satisfied, always insatiable. Hoards of the latter had devastated central Florida. Others were marching toward their final victory—changing the River of Grass into a watery cemetery.

By the time I drove into the parking lot of the Souls Harbor church, nature had declared war on the earth and pelted the ground with watery bullets. I sat behind the steering wheel for a while as the rain drummed on the hood and windshield. What I could make out of the church was multi-layered and multi-colored. It was larger than I had imagined. I guessed the seating capacity was close to seven hundred. In the distance, red letters on a white sign announced it was the future site of a recreation hall.

Rain still pounded on the car as I watched a white Toyota pull up in front of the church. A door opened and a lady fled inside, holding a newspaper over her head to shield her from the drops.

When the storm called a truce, I eased out of the car and raced toward the entrance. Inside, I saw a smiling, young woman behind a desk.

"May I help you, sir?"

"My name is Jarrod Banyon. Is the pastor in?"

She nodded. "He's in his office. May I tell him what this is about?"

"Two members of his congregation have gone missing, and I'm looking for them."

Alarm flashed across her face. I regretted being so dramatic.

After phoning the pastor, she pointed down a carpeted hallway. "The second office on your right, Mr. Banyon."

I thanked her.

The pastor walked from his desk and was at the door to greet me, with an outstretched hand. I shook it.

"Mr. Banyon. I'm Larry Haniford, the pastor here."

"Good to meet you."

"You said something about two members being missing."

After seeing the size of the church I wondered if a pastor would have knowledge of two individual members, but Pastor Haniford offered hope. His youth surprised me. I guessed he was just a few years past thirty. His blond hair sparkled, as did his smile, yet the brown eyes held concern and, I thought, intelligence. He had the pale skin of many native Floridians, with a smattering of golden freckles. His tone was deep baritone.

"Yes, they may have run away."

He gestured to a chair as he walked back around his desk. "Who are we talking about, Mr. Banyon?"

20

"Stephanie Canterley and Ted Landers."

His eyes widened in surprise. "Stephanie and Ted? Are you sure?"

"Her mother said Stephanie left for school yesterday morning, and she hasn't seen her since."

Silently, he placed his arms on the table and interlaced his fingers. "That's shocking. I have talked with Stephanie several times. It was not really counseling, although she has confided in me, but there was nothing in our conversations that led me to believe anything like this would happen."

I was glad to see someone was concerned about Stephanie. His compassion was real, not cooked-up piety. I told him there was another troubling aspect to her disappearance, then mentioned the missing weapons. The alert eyes blinked recognition. His body stiffened.

"Do you know something about guns, pastor?"

He nodded. "My father is a hunter. We often hunted when I was young and also practiced with pistols, although I haven't been out to a range for years."

"Then you realize the Desert Warrior is more of a man's weapon. It's a large gun. The GLC, on the other hand, is a perfect fit for a woman's hand and could be hidden easily in a purse."

He shifted uneasily in his seat, then gave a slight nod.

"Pastor, would they use the guns for any criminal activity?"

"No. Absolutely not. It's inconceivable."

"That would be one explanation for the theft. If that option is out, it leaves the second explanation, which is more troubling than the first."

"I don't quite follow you," he said, but his voice trailed off, as if considering an ominous revelation.

"I was told Stephanie has the knack of handling everything life hands her."

"Yes. Her faith has helped her with that. She is very mature for her age. She was a friendly and optimistic young woman even before she met Christ. Now, you can see the love in her. It's reflected on her face."

"So an intelligent young woman not prone to emotional or reckless behavior grabs two guns—one for her boyfriend and one for herself—but they don't plan on knocking over any liquor stores. I'm guessing she thinks they're in danger and the guns are needed for protection. The question is, what type of danger?"

Pastor Haniford leaned back in his chair as worry lines etched his brow. He reminded me of one of my superiors in Army Intelligence. Major Russer's integrity could cut steel. I sensed the pastor cared about his congregation the way the major cared about his men. I almost called him "sir," a word I don't use a lot. Underneath the freckles he didn't look like the toughest armadillo on the planet—as the major did—but I didn't doubt his strength.

He swallowed hard before answering. "I'm trying to find a flaw in your argument, Mr. Banyon."

"I've tried too. I don't think it's there, although I wouldn't mind being wrong."

After an uneasy silence, he said, "If what you say is true, I would hope Stephanie and Ted would come to me."

"They might not have been able to. Or maybe they felt if they came here, it would put you in danger too."

The worry lines widened a bit.

"I know a little about Stephanie but nothing about Ted. Can you tell me about him?"

"Ted Landers is a fine young man. He has a first-rate mind and an even temperament and many interests."

"What would those interests be?"

"A wide range. He was majoring in chemistry at one time and doing very well, but I think he changed it due to his other interests. He enjoys anthropology and is a history buff. He's always had a deep love for Scripture. He's in his second year at Florida Atlantic University and has gone on several digs in

22

Mexico. I think his IQ is close to the genius level."

"Know where he comes from?"

"Miami. His family is in Dade County. He started attending church here about two years ago and a few months after that came to the altar and accepted Jesus. He's been an outstanding Christian since that time."

"Anything in his behavior recently that—"

Pastor Haniford shook his head. "No, Ted's been a regular churchgoer. Lately, he struck up a friendship with Roy Tibbets, an evangelist who's up here on vacation. Roy's a native Floridian, but his mission field is Central America and southern Mexico. He started a number of successful churches down there. He's something of a history buff too, so his interests coincided with Ted's. Ted was also fascinated by Roy's knowledge of demonology."

"Not the typical field of study."

The pastor smiled. "That may sound strange to the natural mind, but I assure you there are demonic beings and they are stronger in regions where idol worship has been practiced. Some idols can act like a magnet in attracting demonic powers. In Roy's ministry there was even an instance where a demon materialized."

I hoped my smile didn't look patronizing. "He spoke with this minister often?"

The pastor nodded. "After the last several services I always saw Ted talking with Roy, often in very animated conversation."

"Is Rev. Tibbets still in the area?"

"Yes. He's staying here a month before he returns to Central America. One of our members is in real estate and had a house available that Roy is using."

"Could I have the address?"

"Of course." He grabbed a pen and hastily wrote on a calendar pad, then ripped off the sheet and gave it to me. "It's not far— about eight miles from here."

In exchange for the address, I gave him my card. "If either Stephanie or Ted try to contact you, or if you think of something that might help me find them, would you give me a call?"

For a moment he studied me, the brown glare darting up and down. As I had evaluated him, now I was being weighed in the balance. I was mildly curious at what the pastor's judgment would be. He gave an almost imperceptible nod. "I will do my best to help find them, Mr. Banyon."

I thanked him and walked to the door. When my hand grasped the doorknob, his voice stopped me. "We have a number of intercessors at this church. I will ask them to begin praying about this," he said.

I shrugged. It couldn't hurt.

Before leaving, I got Ted's address from the church, but since the minister's residence was closer I decided to talk to Rev. Tibbets first. His house was older than the first two I had entered today, and had an acre of land around it. Two huge oak trees shaded the house. The lawn was a dull lime green but neat and trim. It was a two-story, wooden residence, with the top story looking smaller than the first floor. I breathed a sigh of relief. No ceramic objects or gold door knockers. On the faded blue porch, two white chairs guarded the screen door.

I stopped the car in the empty driveway and got out. Climbing the two steps to the porch, I then knocked on the door. Sounds of a television came from within. I knocked again. When I moved to the left, I spied a large, overstuffed gold chair. An arm hung down, with the fingers close to the wooded, dusty floor, but I couldn't see the rest of the man.

The door wasn't locked. I opened it and stepped inside.

"Rev. Tibbets?"

There was no response. I walked into the living room. Some obscure talk show was on the tube, but Rev. Tibbets wasn't listening.

Perhaps the evangelist had battled demonic entities and had even seen one with his physical eyes, but his last adversary had not been ethereal. The single bullet in his head had been fired by a flesh-and-blood hand. Two lines of red flowed around Rev. Tibbets' nose and spotted his yellow shirt. The shooter had not been perfect. The bullet was not right between the eyes but a millimeter off to the right. I guessed the assailant had stood in the kitchen doorway, about fifteen feet from his victim.

I took out my Glock and looked around, but everything was still. Whoever had killed Rev. Tibbets was long gone. I wasn't going to waste time mourning. If what he preached was right, then he was in heaven, but Stephanie was still on Earth, and in danger.

The Scriptures state David took five smooth stones. Stephanie took two guns. David knew what he was up against. Did Stephanie know what she was up against? God had been with David. Perhaps He'd be with Stephanie too.

Not being a Christian I had no revelation, only human instinct. My instinct told me Rev. Tibbets wouldn't be the only death in this case. It also told me someone wanted Stephanie dead. And whoever it was wanted to place Ted in the grave right next to hers.

Four

I phoned the Flagler County Sheriff's Department, then tried to wait patiently for the officers. In the movies or television, the private detective often plays fast and loose with police. It's a good plot device to have him at odds with the local authorities as well as the criminals. In real life, that's not a real good plan. The state can yank your license if you have a casual attitude toward the law. Plus, I knew several detectives in the Volusia County Sheriff's Department and trusted them. We got along well. The Flagler County staff I wasn't sure of, but I was hoping for the best.

The tan patrol car pulled into the driveway a few minutes later, and a tall, solid brick wall of a deputy got out. He wore a crewcut and tainted yellow shades. A toothpick was stuck in his mouth. The sun bounced lasers off his badge and gold nameplate. Although as pale as Pastor Haniford, he looked like he'd be more comfortable in a forest than in a pew. He walked toward me.

"In here, deputy," I said. "When I walked in the house I found the body. I didn't move or touch anything."

I followed him in. He stood in the doorway, chewed on the toothpick, then turned my way. "Are you Mr. Banyon? The man who called this in?"

"Yes."

"Would you wait outside, sir? I'll talk to you in a minute."

I nodded and stepped out. I stayed on the porch, in the shade, until the second car pulled in. A uniformed officer was behind the wheel, but the man who stepped out of the passenger side wore a brown suit and tie. He was older than the deputy. Law-enforcement people are in a tough field that is getting tougher every day, but not all look grim as if weighed down by human depravity. This man had a bright smile. His eyes flashed intelligence and gaiety. At the same time, there was a no-nonsense manner about him.

As he climbed the steps he looked at me and asked if I was Banyon. I said I was.

"Be with you in a minute," he said.

I heard the rustle of conversation. In a minute or so, the second deputy walked to his car and grabbed his radio. When he hung it back up, an ambulance slid into view.

My gaze stayed on the three EMTs who eased the stretcher out. Then I felt the gentle tug on my shoulder. "Mr. Banyon. Identification says the victim is named Roy Tibbets. Is that who you were looking for?"

"Yes."

He guided me toward the end of the porch, giving the EMTs plenty of room as they approached. He reached into his coat pocket and brought out a mini-recorder, as well as a rectanglar reporter's notebook.

"I like to record conversations. I take notes, but sometimes I have trouble reading my own handwriting. Ever have that problem?"

"All the time," I said.

Which was true in my case. I had a hunch his writing was precise and that he was meticulous about crossing his T's and dotting his I's. The detective extended his hand. "My name is Webb Owen. Been with the force almost twenty years now."

"Good to meet you, Detective," I said as I shook his hand.

A red button flickered as he switched the recorder on. "Would you mind telling me why you were looking for Mr. Tibbets? I assume, Mr. Banyon, that you have a permit for the gun you're carrying?"

27

"Yes, I do," I said quickly. "I can show it to you." I had assumed the coat covered the holster perfectly.

I guess not to a veteran policeman.

His eyes seemed to dance as he smiled. "We'll get to that later. Take the first question."

"I'm a private detective. I was hired to find a young Volusia County woman named Stephanie Canterley. She's a possible runaway with her boyfriend. Both go to Souls Harbor, which is a church a few miles from here. I was told the boyfriend—a student named Ted Landers—had formed a friendship with Rev. Tibbets. I was wondering if he might guess where they had gone."

"The deceased is a reverend?"

"A missionary who was back in the area for about a month."

"A runaway couple?"

I nodded. "Possibly. I can't confirm Ted is with her, but that's my assumption."

"Know why they left?"

"Not yet." I swallowed. "There is something you should know, Detective, although I don't think it has anything to do with the murder. Stephanie and Ted may be armed. Her father is a collector, and he said he was missing two guns. One was a Fobus GLC."

A ripple of interest flowed in his eyes. Like the reverend, he knew about guns.

I continued. "I notice the bullet that killed Rev. Tibbets...."

Owen nodded. "Came from a small handgun. Possibly a GLC."

"I can't believe these two had any part in murder."

The detective smiled as if he had just spied a murder suspect with a smoking gun. "You'd be surprised what young people do nowadays. Did you hear about that case up in Duval eight, maybe nine months ago? Two males were killed in a fight about a female. One shot the other. The second managed to knife the shooter before he died. Know how old they were? Twelve. Know how old the female was? Eleven."

"This isn't like that."

"Well, we'll see. Why don't you show me your license?"

I opened my coat very slowly, reached into the pocket to pull out my state-certified piece of paper, and handed it to him.

He looked it over. "Volusia County?"

"Yes."

"I know some officers down there. If I called them, what would they say about you, Mr. Banyon?"

"That my heart is pure but that I have a lousy golf swing."

He chuckled. "Who specifically would say that?"

I gave him some names. He flipped the license over, then stared at it. "Is this still your home address?"

I nodded.

He handed the license back to me. "Nice to meet you."

Five

I drove slowly back to Volusia County, the home of sun, sand, beaches, and spring-breakers. But my mind wasn't on those subjects. I wondered what motive could have prompted Rev. Tibbets' killer. If the pastor was correct—and I had no reason to think he was mistaken or lying—most of the reverend's time was spent out of the country. Who up here would know him, or have any reason to kill him? Mistake? No. Whoever killed him had taken aim at his target. Burglary gone bad? Doubtful. I hadn't had time to check the house, but I didn't think anything was missing.

I briefly pondered returning to the Canterleys and asking the jolly couple if Stephanie had any enemies. But certainly they would have mentioned it if they thought so. Or would they? I could see them pitching themselves in front of the idol to save it from a sledgehammer, but sacrificing for their daughter...?

Ted Landers' address was in the western part of the county so the sides of the road leading to his residence were not just walls of concrete. A few remaining county trees, their numbers devastated by the battle against urbanization, stood out starkly and sadly against the horizon. The branches were bare of leaves and offered up to the sky as if in surrender. The road was still wet and slick with rain. The sky rumbled. In the distance, lightning flashed and flew toward the ground.

I knew the approximate area but made at least one wrong turn, then hit Abner Avenue. It took me to a cul-de-sac with two blue-and-white and two orange-and-brown duplexes. The first one had a wooden sign on a post designating the manager. Behind it, a woman in a green blouse and jeans watered a clump of rose bushes. I got out and extended greetings. She nodded.

"I'm looking for the residence of Ted Landers," I said.

She squeezed the nozzle to cut the water off, then wiped her wet hands on her jeans. The stare was one of curiosity with a hint of suspicion.

"Ted. The best tenant I've got," she said.

She was middle-aged, with a short mass of red curly hair, a quick smile, and deep gray eyes. She walked over to the spigot and began to roll up the hose. "He's helpful, sweet, and pays the rent on time. Wish he was my son. So many young people today are crude. Foul language. Obscene manners. Grabbing themselves and cursing. They think they're entitled to a living. We know better, don't we...I didn't catch your name."

That was because I hadn't given it. I reached into my pocket and brought out my identification. "Jarrod Banyon. I'm a private detective."

"Mine's Alma Randolph," she said as she walked toward the house. She sat down on the front steps and glared at me. "I can't believe Ted is in any kind of trouble."

"Well, ma'am, he's missing."

"Missing?"

I nodded. I reached in my pocket again and brought out the picture of Stephanie. "Have you ever seen this girl around?"

She looked at it and nodded. "Yes. That's his girlfriend. Met her a couple of times. She's real sweet. They make a lovely couple. Is she missing too?"

"Yes. I'm trying to find them before they get into any trouble, or before trouble finds them."

"Parents hire you?" she asked.

"Yes," I said, although I didn't specify which group of parents.

She looked concerned about Ted, so I took a chance. "Ms.

Randolph—"

"Call me Alma."

I smiled. "Alma, there's something else. A man has just been killed up in Flagler County. He was known to both Stephanie and Ted. I don't think they had anything to do with it, but the police may want to question them. Stephanie just had a fight with her parents before she and Ted took off. I think they may be frightened and angry. The sooner I can find them, the better."

Alma gave me the Pastor Haniford stare. I hoped my grace and charm would impress her. Or possibly that the pastor's intercessory prayer people would help swing her my way.

"I haven't seen Ted today or for most of yesterday," Alma said. "I'd like to be of help, Mr. Banyon, but—"

"Please call me Jarrod. I was wondering if I might look at his apartment."

She gave me another stern, questioning stare, then stood up. A worried look replaced the inquisitive one. "I'd like to help Jarrod but...even a landlord is not supposed to enter an apartment without permission..."

"Aren't there exceptions in cases of emergencies? I think Ted would appreciate it and understand."

Either my persuasiveness or the prayers worked.

"Come with me," she said.

Ted had the west-side apartment almost directly across from hers. There were two deck chairs outside. She inserted a key in his door. It clicked as she unlocked it. She glanced back with a furtive look. "Let's just keep this between you and me."

"I will."

She pushed the door open. "Just come back and let me know when you're through."

I thanked her.

The apartment was one of the ones trimmed in blue and white and it had a similar interior. White carpets, blue furniture, blue cabinets in the kitchen. I thought I saw a woman's touch in the few decorative flourishes. Two vases of flowers, two Daytona seaside paintings that I didn't think came with the apartment. Perhaps the cleanliness belied a woman's touch too, although I had known a few men who were neat freaks. Neat freak is not a category I fit into. I've had a girlfriend or two who complained of my slovenliness.

The rooms were spic-and-span, dust-free. I checked out a calendar hanging on the wall. Neat, blue handwriting appeared on several blocks of days. Several books were on a small coffee table in the living room. One textbook was opened with a pencil in the crease. A number of lines had been underlined in green ink. A desk with a computer sat next to another end table full of books. I moved to the bedroom and spied a gold-framed picture of Stephanie on a dresser drawer. She wore a yellow blouse and had a yellow ribbon tying back her hair. Her smile could have warmed the city. There was a Bible on the night table. I skimmed it and saw there was more than one passage underlined with the same green marker that had been used in the textbook.

I drew a closet door back and looked in on an array of student clothes. I pushed back some shirts and smiled as a green-and-white Dolphin jacket came into view. Landers was from Miami, but he was in Jacksonville Jaguar territory now. A few shirts down was a Florida Marlins T-shirt. The boy was a sports fan. I slid the closet door shut. Since he was from Miami, would he return and talk to his parents, assuming his parents were more of the typical, helpful variety than the Canterleys?

I opened some drawers, feeling slightly guilty when I did. But I didn't know what I was looking for and wouldn't until I found it. The bottom drawer creaked when I slid it opened. I smiled. Not everything is digital. I took the half-dozen pictures and sat back on the bed.

More photos of Stephanie. Nothing gaudy or sleazy, but there was one of her in an orange bikini. It was about as modest as a bikini could be. Beads of water appeared on her neck, shoulders, and face. I wasn't foolish enough to think there was a contradiction between the Bible on the bedstand and a bikinied Stephanie photo. Even if I were twenty-one and full of faith, I'd have enjoyed looking at Stephanie in a two-piece. There was also a picture of her in a Dolphin T-shirt, with her arm up as if tossing a pass. Bare legs, but I assumed there was something beneath the shirt. She had the five-star Stephanie smile. I was more interested in the next photo. It was the first sight I had of Ted.

He stood with his left arm around Stephanie's shoulders while she had her arm around his waist. Both of them looked totally in love. Ted's gaze on her was adoring. Hers was way past affectionate.

He was about six-foot, brown-haired, broad-shouldered. I had mentally placed him as a geek. The brown eyes appeared studious, intelligent. But those archaeological digs had developed biceps.

I returned the photos to the drawer. The wood rustled as I closed it. I wondered again what would make the couple bolt and run.

I flicked on the computer, then walked to the calendar again. I looked more closely at the writing. Among other notations, Ted scribbled twice that he had a meeting with Rev. Tibbetts, one at nine and another at three, but he had not written where.

The computer blinked on and, fortunately, he didn't use a password. I looked at the choices and hit My Documents. Little pages flicked into view. I ignored most of them but placed the cursor on Spir-Da. Knowing Ted's background, I hoped that meant spiritual diary.

It did.

The diary was a lot longer and more detailed than I expected. I saw Stephanie's name often and a frequent use of Rev. Tibbets' name. At least one other item struck me as alarming. The mention of Chad Atkinson puzzled me. The prior boyfriend of Stephanie rated some good lines in Ted's account. There was also the cryptic line "C may be in some danger...wants to get out."

I needed more time than a brief read on a computer screen.

As the pages printed out and dropped neatly into the wire container, I walked over to the door and peeked out the window. No one was in sight. I returned to the printer, folded up the two dozen pages, and slid them into my coat pocket.

I checked a small bookcase in the hall. Landers was an avid reader. There were books on history, current affairs, and a number of religious titles. On the kitchen table, there was also a book rack. I skimmed the titles and one caught my eye. I pulled it out and opened it, seeing the omnipresent green liner. Landers had also scribbled notes with blue ink in the margin.

I closed the book to check the title again and turned it over. It was a history of the occult by a British professor currently at Oxford. I wondered why a young Christian would be reading about the occult. Know the enemy? I remembered the line by Oliver North that every morning he read the Bible and *The Washington Post*. That way he knew what both sides were saying.

I eased down in a chair to study the passages underlined in green, with Landers' own blue scribbling at the side of the page. The chapter "Idol Worship" had a full-page picture of a figurine almost as ugly as the one taken from the Danielsons. I didn't know quite what to make of the first few pages of the chapter. Perhaps I should take the book to Pastor Haniford and ask his comments. I ripped out several pages, then folded and placed them next to the computer printouts in my pocket. I was getting loaded down.

On my way back to my car, I thanked Alma for her help.

"See anything that indicates where they might be?"

"Maybe. I'm not sure yet," I said.

"I certainly would like to help."

I gave her my card and told her if she remembered anything that might be of help to give me a call.

Affection for Ted had brightened her eyes, but now a grim shade of gray dimmed her vision. She shook her head. "They're such good kids. Why do good kids have so much trouble?"

They meet up with bad people...or have bad parents, I thought.

While driving back to the city, I called an acquaintance, Ronald Meadows, and asked if I could buy him a late lunch. Meadows is one of the vice-presidents of the local chamber of commerce and has extensive knowledge of local businesses. As I drove to the restaurant I phoned the Canterleys' bank. When I was transferred to an earnest young man, I told him I had a rather large check from a Bolly Canterley. I had no prior association with Mr. Canterley, so I wondered if he had money to cover it. The young man did not have to check the account when I told him the amount.

"I assure you that Mr. Canterley has more than enough to cover that check, and ten like it," he said in a snippish tone.

"Thank you," I said. "Could you also tell me what business Mr. Canterley is in? Our business involved the purchase of services, and I did not even ask him what he did for a living."

"Real estate," came the immediate reply. "One of the most successful realtors in the county, but he doesn't like the limelight so he has always been a bit in the shadows. I believe he has now made forays into land development and has been very successful."

I thanked him again. I was glad to hear Canterley was more than solvent but still wasn't going to waste time depositing his check. I used the drive-in lane at my bank on the way to the restaurant.

When I entered, Meadows was at a corner table sipping a whiskey sour. He waved as I walked over and stuck out his hand.

"Jarrod. How's business?"

"Got a new case this morning."

He smiled. "So that's what this is about."

I nodded. We both ordered the luncheon special, me without bothering to check what it was. I asked the waiter to bring a second whiskey sour to the table. I met Meadows a few years ago when I did a favor for the chamber. Since that time, the officers have been friendly and appreciative.

"So what can I do for you, Jarrod? Need business advice?"

"Of a sort. Know anything about antiques, Ron?"

"I know I'm rapidly becoming one."

I chuckled. "I'm interested in a husband-and-wife team who run Sea Island Galleries. The husband is not all that likeable a character. Know anything about them?"

He didn't answer immediately. He picked up his drink and swirled the liquor around in the glass. While he was still shaking the drink, a waiter arrived and brought the special, which was a hot roast-beef sandwich. When the smell of hot roast beef hit me, I realized I had not eaten since very early in the morning. I cut a piece and swallowed it while Meadows swirled his drink.

"Yeah, Danielson is a nice guy, isn't he? Does the chamber add a 10 percent surcharge for a member who's a jackass?" I said

37

as I woofed down bread and beef.

Meadows took a swallow and set the drink back on the table. "Mr. Gary Danielson is one of our fine, local businessmen who care deeply about our community. He has often given to local charities."

"Of course. Now that you have dutifully given me the official chamber line on a member, what's the real story on him?"

"He's an obnoxious, fat jerk." Meadows grabbed his fork and knife and began cutting into his sandwich. "He has always paid his chamber fees on time but usually stays away from meetings, which is all right with me. When he has attended, he has usually argued with another member."

"I gather the wife is the brains of the outfit."

He nodded. "She has made him rich."

"How rich are they? Are they experiencing any financial troubles?"

"Not that I know of, but I'm not their accountant. In the antique business, sometimes you take risks that don't pay off."

"Any shadowy rumors surrounding the dear couple?"

He swallowed a large forkful of beef, then washed it down by draining his glass. He signaled the waiter for another drink. "Why do you care, Jarrod? How are they involved with you?"

"I'm tracking a teenage runaway who may have taken off with one of their beloved ugly idols. The teen is a friend of their daughter, who was obviously switched at birth from another family."

He nodded. "I've met Tiffany too. She's an argument against sterilization. Lovely girl. My son goes to the same high school as her. Cliff has asked her out several times, but she's always turned him down."

"She has battled depression and might not have been in the mood for a date."

He stopped slicing away at his lunch. "I didn't know that.

Cliff told me she'd turned down a lot of guys, but I figured that was just his ego fibbing a bit."

Meadows was silent for a moment. I thought he was trying to avoid the question but, after taking another swig of his drink, he said, "The Danielsons have made no friends in the chamber. They don't go around trying to win friends and influence people but, as far as I know, they don't have any felonies on their record." He paused again, then added, "Officially."

"Officially? And unofficially?"

He scratched the corner of his lips. "In confidence?"

I nodded.

"The Danielsons deal in artifacts that are often difficult and time-consuming to obtain, but are very valuable once they're in the antique shop. There are rumors that the cheery couple are not choosy in how they get those objects. They don't mind dealing with some very shady characters who happen to own, or have at least acquired, those objects."

"Gosh, you could have fooled me," I said. "I would have sworn they were upright and law-abiding."

"Understand, there has been no criminal investigation of the Danielsons, but the shop has been the center of an occasional ugly rumor. Of course, any law-enforcement inquiry would be countered with reasonable explanations. The objects they have on display are not illegal. So when a person shows up with an artifact, there is no reason to ask where or how it was obtained. Such objects are scattered across Mexico, Central and South America. It's not illegal to find them, or sell them."

"Even so, I gather you would not do business with them?"

"I would not, nor would I have any extended social contact with them, even if they desired it."

I took another bite of the sandwich. "Would you do business with Bolly Canterley?"

He raised his glass. "Another one of our fine members."

"Yes, but you can skip the official intro."

"Bolly Canterley is more sociable than Danielson. He and his wife attend our meetings and an occasional social function. He's considered to be a very shrewd businessman who has made some very good guesses and, from time to time, has been very lucky."

"Lucky? What do you mean?"

"Well, for example, a dozen or so years ago, he and a few other investors wanted to develop Sea Turtle Acres. It's a development close to the Flagler County line. Trouble is, an old-time native Floridian owned about five, six acres of the parcel the development group wanted. It was a huge development, but Cyphus Sexton had his half-dozen acres right in the center of it. He hated all the new growth in the state. He grew up when Florida was rural and liked the streams, the lakes, the forests, and the nature trails."

"So do I."

"Cyphus wasn't about to sell. He didn't need the money, and he enjoyed preventing a new development. Canterley and his friends were stymied. Then Cyphus died."

That stopped my fork halfway to my mouth. "Really. Anything—"

Meadows shook his head. "There was no evidence of foul play. Cyphus was elderly. He was thought to be in good health but was pushing eighty. Might have been even older. Doctors believe his heart just quit one night while he was sleeping."

"His heirs sell?"

"Yes. His son inherited the six acres, among other things. For a while, it looked like he might be as obstinate as his dad. Then he started having some financial problems, so he sold. A stroke of luck for the investors." He took a sip of his third drink. "It wasn't the first time luck, or fate, seemed to favor the Canterleys."

I frowned. Luck, or fate, didn't seem to be favoring their daughter. Perhaps, like schizophrenia, it skipped a generation.

"Know anything about their daughter, Stephanie?"

"No. Never met her."

The waiter brought the check. I grabbed it and thanked Meadows. As I stood up, he said, "There's one more thing, Jarrod."

I sat down again.

"Check with Kevin Nadler."

"The retired county detective?"

He nodded. "It was so long ago that I've forgotten the details, but I vaguely recall that, one time, a nasty rumor popped up about the Danielsons. I don't remember much about the story. It must have been eight, nine years ago. Nadler might know all the details."

"Thank you, Ron. You're a good man."

Back in my car, I dialed Tiffany's cell-phone number. Her enthusiastic voice was the bright spot of the day.

"Mr. Banyon. Any news of Stephanie and Ted?"

"Not yet," I told her. Then I asked if she knew of any place that the couple might go to, a place maybe only they and she knew about. She said nothing came to mind, but she would think about it and call me back.

Six

I had returned to my office, poured a Coke, and was reading Landers' diary when the phone rang. I thought it might be Tiffany, but Alma Randolph's voice came on the line. She said she wasn't sure, but she might have a clue to the whereabouts of Ted and Stephanie. She said it was a long shot, but I agreed to drive out and speak to her.

Alma Randolph opened the door as I pulled into her driveway. She held it open as I walked into the apartment.

"Would you like some coffee or tea?"

I requested tea as I sat down.

"Cold or hot?"

"Cold, please, with a little extra sugar."

She brought me a tall glass. I sipped it and enjoyed the flavor. Alma sat across the room in a rocking chair. "I may have to apologize for bringing you out here. After I called you, I had doubts this would be of any help at all."

I smiled. "Since I'm here, tell me what's on your mind."

She eased back in the chair. "This happened about a month after I first saw Stephanie. Ted had packed up a small suitcase and said he was going on a church retreat. This was on a Wednesday. That next Sunday evening I went out for my evening walk—it was later than usual—and noticed both Ted and Stephanie were sitting outside Ted's apartment. I walked over and said hello. Apparently, Stephanie had gone on the retreat too and they both were raving about it: the sermons were great, the scenery was breathtaking, the people they met were friendly. They both said they experienced great growth as Christians, and both said they wanted to return, if not on another religious retreat, then at least to the location."

I nodded.

"The meeting place was over in the Panhandle, in Walton County."

"One of the few places in the state where there are no condos, as yet," I said, "although I haven't been there for about three years. Some developer might have erected one since then."

"I remember they said the meeting was held at Shady Oaks Fellowship. It was surrounded by a forest but had all the modern conveniences. I think some denomination had created it to be a retreat for ministers or church officials. If Stephanie and Ted are on the run and wanted a quite place to stay and think, and be safe..."

"Yes, it sounds like a good place to hide," I said.

"I don't know if you think it's worth checking out."

"Yes, I do. It was a place of joy and safety for them. In a time of stress, they might want to return there." I drained the remainder of the tea and placed the glass on the TV stand. "Thank you, Alma."

While I was driving back to the city, Bolly Canterley called on my cell phone. His voice seemed both frenzied, yet also diffident.

"Mr. Banyon?"

"I'm here."

"Mr. Banyon, one of the officers at my bank just called. He was inquiring if there was anything wrong."

"Why would he think that?"

"Yesterday, Stephanie came in and cashed a thousand-dollar

43

check. He said he saw her and said hello, but she rushed out. He said a young man was with her. Later, he checked her account and found a three-hundred-dollar ATM withdrawal—that's the most the bank allows in one day—that was made later in the afternoon."

"Did he say where the withdrawal was made?"

"At a convenience store near St. Augustine. They could be heading north."

"Yes," I said. "I'll go after them."

I didn't tell Canterley that the young couple might be heading north but only to get to Interstate 10 in Jacksonville. I-10 headed west into the Panhandle and went through Walton County.

Seven

Thanks to the Internet and a couple of phone calls, it wasn't difficult to pinpoint the location of the Shady Oaks facility. It was established by the Southern Baptists about twenty years ago to use for conferences, seminars, and summer school camps in rural Walton County. There was one large church, complete with meeting rooms, plus a half-dozen cabins to house students during the camps, a cafeteria, and a few storage sheds.

I packed a small suitcase, my overnight shaving kit, and a briefcase, where I placed Landers' diary and the pages I'd torn from his book. Instead of driving north, I headed out State Road 40. It would take me through the Ocala National Forest to the city of Ocala, where I would turn north on Interstate 75. Interstate 75 would connect with Interstate 10 just north of Lake City.

I had driven through the Ocala National Forest many times and had walked through it many times. It used to be a rather desolate stretch of road from Ormund Beach to Ocala. Not anymore. At one time, there was one restaurant in the middle part of the stretch. It was convenient for meals and, once when my stomach turned over and twisted in digestive distress, for a needed call of nature. Long ago.

I lamented again the sad demise of my native state. The ugly, urban sprawl is a cancer, sucking the life out of the sunshine vibrancy. The condos along the shorelines are white hilts of cement knives wounding the land, leaving it bleeding

45

from a thousand cuts. The tacky shops and stores have spread like infections. The green lands and forests, once pristine and beautiful, are being squeezed and lost. The deer and quail and the manatees are fighting a losing battle, slowly being decimated as more and more humans trample on their environment.

Perhaps we should build a monument to growth. Instead of the pure streams and breathtaking valleys, we could create a concrete waterfall and an asphalt river. Sure, scenic wonders would be lost, but the state would gain an ever-endless stream of Taco Bells. I'm not sure that's a fair trade.

I grew up in a small town surrounded by forest and streams. I tracked the deer, walked the forest paths, fished in the ponds, and surfed on the beaches. No animal—whether bear, cougar, or Florida panther—ever frightened me. Yes, they were dangerous and they could kill, but the trees and the hills and the lands were theirs. It was their home, and they roamed as friends and companions. I never felt fear, not in their lands, perhaps because I respected their terrain.

In fact, from the time I could walk I frightened my mother by rushing toward large dogs to pet them. German shepherds, Dobermans, even pit bulls—I'd run and throw my arms around them. I still remember my mother's anguished scream when, as a five-year-old, I grabbed a growling Wolfhound. But it calmed down and starting playing with me. I've always had a way with animals.

I still remember turning down a path and seeing a black panther on the edge of a fallen tree limb. He barred his teeth and growled. I smiled and eased my way around him and waved in homage as I circled. He growled again, this time in a lower note, a deep rumbling in his throat.

I've swum with the manatees, those ugly yet graceful creatures of the sea, and met a lovely lady kayaker who gave tours to tourists and locals at Cocoa Beach Kayaking. The adorable "Kack" gave each manatee on her route a name and, amazingly enough, some responded to her melodic tone. She is a manatee whisperer and the creatures hone in to her gentle tones. She, too, like Ted and Stephanie, is a Christian. Manatees reflected the beauty of God's creation to her. It was man who brought ugliness and violence to the world. Once I noticed odd markings on a manatee. When I swam closer I saw that some reprobate had carved his initials into the manatee's back.

If I'm ever elected king or overlord, I will not abolish the death penalty. I will expand it. That knife-wielding moral moron will be the first to be strung up. No appeals. No objections that the execution might cause undue distress to the victim. When death is involved, you expect a bit of discomfort.

Drastic? Perhaps. But nobody would mistreat manatees in my kingdom. Or any other animal for that matter. If you don't like the rules, stay away. In addition to the severe punishments for hurting manatees, this overlord would mandate strict zoning restrictions and low-density requirements.

Of course, the condos, the shops, the concrete are only symptoms of the disease that's killing Florida. The problem is there are simply too many people. When my father grew up, there were three million people in the Sunshine State. There are now more than twenty million. In the year 2000, the state's population was fifteen point nine million. Six years later, the nineteen million mark had been surpassed and the numbers were still rolling. Three-plus million in just six years, with no sign of stopping. New people mean new houses, new asphalt, new power plants, new schools, and tons and tons of new trash. They have put their initials on the state the way that watery sadist marked the manatee, leaving only ugliness, squalor, and pain.

That night I stayed at a motel in Lake City. Usually I don't mind driving way into the night. I'm more of a night person. I don't like mornings. It takes me three cups of coffee to get settled and awake in the mornings. I make up for the time I lose in the morning traveling by spending extra time on the road at night. But a weariness hampered me today so I stopped early. It was difficult to believe that it was only this morning I had arrived at the Canterleys' doorstep, walking under the malignant, angry ceramic god to enter their home.

A steak house provided a high-quality Porterhouse, a delicious baked potato, and a crisp, fresh salad. After dinner I retired to the room and began reading Ted's notes. I appreciated that he had a good command of the language and was concerned with other things than noting how hot his girlfriend was. The peripheral remarks about Stephanie were couched in a romantic, not lustful, tone. I hadn't met the young man yet but, reading his thoughts, I increasingly gained respect for him.

A Daytona Beach station was listed on the motel's TV list so I switched it on to hear the eleven o'clock news. I was hoping to not hear a specific story, but the Rev. Tibbets report was second on the broadcast. I grimaced.

The reporter, a tall, dark-haired man with glasses, seemed rather competent, something you can't always say about other members of his profession. He told viewers a missionary from the area, Rev. Roy Tibbets, had been killed by a single shot to the head. The Rev. Tibbets had arrived from Central America for a vacation but planned to return to his mission field at the end of the month. While in Florida, he was attending Souls Harbor, one of his sponsoring churches. There was a brief comment from Pastor Haniford about how shocking the murder was.

There were no suspects in the case, the reporter said, but the Flagler County Sheriff's Department did have two "persons of interest" they wanted to question.

Those two, I had no doubt, were Stephanie and Ted.

I propped the pillows up, stretched out, and returned to Ted's diary. I dropped the pages from the occult history on the bed too. As I flipped open a page of the dairy, I was drowsy, but the next two long paragraphs woke me up and straightened the hairs on the back of my neck. I read them over and over again, then went line by line across the remaining pages. I picked up the torn book leaflets and read them. I didn't know what to think. The young man was speculating based on events and items he had described in his diary. But his conclusion was grisly. What he feared was unimaginable. Romantic delusions? Paranoia? Christianity mixed with a persecution complex? But no one had suggested Landers was mentally troubled. The rest of the diary did not hint of any emotional problems.

I took a deep breath. What if it were true? What it those blue scribblings were not the rant of a mentally disturbed mind but the reasoned and intelligent guesses of a young man frightened for the girl he loved.

Then an ancient evil had come back to haunt the earth. And Ted and Stephanie were right in its path.

Eight

The dreams were bad. Instead of the forests I knew —places of safety and sanctuary—the trees became black and alive, with claws on the ends of the branches that lashed out as I dodged for cover. I stumbled into a city, but the windows of the condos mutated into jagged teeth that opened to devour me.

I woke up gasping for air. I breathed heavily and felt the cold sweat dripping onto my chest.

A shower helped dissipate the gray cloud. Two cups of coffee stimulated brain and body. I decided I would carefully read Landers' writing again in the cold light of day. See if I could find any flaw in his theories. Any logical flaw. I wanted to dismiss his views out of hand. But if he was right, the type of reason I thought I knew, and depended on, was more limited than I had ever imagined.

I had repacked my shaving kit when the cell phone rang. I glanced at the number and saw it was Alma again. I picked it up and said hello.

"Jarrod, thank goodness I got you."

I didn't like the anxiety in her voice. "What's wrong?"

"Two men were just here looking for Ted and Stephanie."

"Policemen?"

"No. They didn't say who they were, but they were asking questions about Ted. Wanted to know if I knew where he was."

"Did you tell them anything?"

"No. I told them I hadn't seen Ted for two days and didn't

know where he was. They wanted to see his apartment. I said no, it was illegal to let anyone in, unless they were policemen and had a warrant. That backed them off for a minute. Then they got a bit nasty so I told them to take off. They didn't like it, but they left, and I called the police."

"Good. Did those men say why they wanted to talk to Ted?"

"No. I asked them, but they didn't answer directly. Just said they were friends, which was clearly a lie."

"What did they look like?"

"One was tall, almost as tall as you. He's white with dirty, black, curly hair. The other was smaller and Hispanic. He spoke with an accent. Wore a gold chain around his neck. Saw a large tattoo of a spider on his forearm."

I frowned and scratched my jaw. "You own a gun, Alma?"

"No, but I have a friend who does. He has two guns actually, and he's a darn good shot."

"Good, why don't you go stay with him for a few days. There's no question in my mind that, if your two visitors thought you knew where Ted was, they would have used violence to make you tell."

There was a long pause on the other end of the line. When she spoke again, the words came slowly. "That was my feeling. I was very glad I was outside when we talked, and that there were witnesses around, near the other apartments. Oh, and there's one other thing. The police were here too, soon after you left."

"Would that be a Detective Owen?"

"Yes."

"Good. In this case, I want the police sniffing around. Did Owen ask to see the apartment?"

"Yes, and I let him in. I mentioned you had been around too. I'm sorry if that—"

"No," I told her. "That's fine. Now I suggest you go see your friend and stay there for a while."

"I'll head out now. I didn't like the looks of those men."

"Alma..."

"Yes."

"If it comes to this, tell your friend not to hesitate. Tell him to shoot to kill."

She closed up the phone. I was standing before the mirror. I could feel the weight of the Glock beneath my armpit, but I lifted the jacket to make sure it was there. I took the Beretta I had placed in one of the motel's drawers and eased it into the ankle holster.

I always like to have a backup plan.

As I rushed to my car, I realized I had changed my mind about Pastor Haniford's intercessors. I no longer dismissed them out of hand. Now I hoped they knew what they were doing and, just on the off chance that Ted was right, I sincerely hoped they were good at their jobs.

It took seven hours before I entered Walton County, thanks in part to a five-car pileup on the I-75 westbound lane. I had a rough idea of the location of Shady Oaks. After I grabbed a quick hamburger at a fast-food joint, I headed out into the county. The city and shops and convenience stores faded, then only trees and trails fenced the two-lane road. It took about ten minutes to negotiate the curves that led me to the rectangular green sign with the small arrow indicating it was eight miles to the Shady Oaks Retreat. There were a number of sharp curves before I saw a clearing. The receding sun bathed the buildings in an odd orange glow. I paused and then, perhaps due to an excess of caution, backed the car up until I found a small opening on the side of the road. I drove the car into it and parked, making sure the car couldn't be seen by passing drivers.

I went the rest of the way on foot. I didn't see a car at first, but as I walked closer, I spied a fender. One of the buildings all but obscured the rest of the Pontiac. I looked around. The area seemed empty. Most of the buildings were self-contained. But one had only a roof and support posts. A long table stretched beneath the roof. I assumed it was for open air meals. I walked to the car, slipped down, and attached the little gadget under the fender. It was almost obsolete in the ultra-high-tech society we have now, but the device was dependable. Always have a backup plan. Just in case.

Darkness slowly covered the facility, but there was a light in one building. I moved closer and edged by the sign designating it as the church. A wisp of musical notes breezed past in the wind. I checked the front door. It was unlocked, so I opened it and slipped into the sanctuary. I heard music and song from inside.

The ground floor was of a semi-circle configuration. I moved around the perimeter of the floor, still in the dark. A row of lights lit up the sanctuary. At a small piano sat Stephanie Canterley, singing beautifully. The pictures didn't do her justice. The overhead lights shone down and gave a peaceful, serene glow around her. Slightly to her right was Ted.

"Hold on my child. Joy comes in the morning..."

If invited to join in, even angels would have politely refused, knowing they could not match her melodic brilliance. I was still some distance away, but I noticed light reflecting from the moisture on her cheeks. A lone tear slid down her jaw and dropped on the yellow carpet.

"Weep-ing only lasts for a while. Hold on—"

I trusted joy would come in the morning, but the song didn't say which morning. I walked closer to the duo, wondering if they would spot me, but Stephanie focused on her singing and Ted looked directly at her. When she finished the song, her fingers glided over the keys and brought a familiar harmony. I have a Baptist background. Mom went regularly. Dad a bit more intermittently. I never rejected my semi-religious upbringing. I just gradually slipped away. But I'd heard "Whispering Hope" too many times to forget it.

Ted tried to do harmony. He knew the words, but he couldn't carry a tune in a basket.

The flow of her tears increased, but it didn't change the sublime majesty of her voice. "*Then when the night is upon us. Why should the heart sink away?*" I thought the remaining lyrics might be a good entrance line. It had been a while since I sang. I took a deep breath. I stepped out of the shadows and joined my baritone to Stephanie's alto.

"*When the dark midnight is over, watch for the breaking of day.*"

Ted, shocked, reached for the gun in the waistband of his pants.

"Ted, no!" Stephanie yelled.

Nervous, he fumbled with the gun.

I grabbed it from him. "Don't be scared, son," I said. I handed the gun back to him. "I'm on your side."

Nine

Stephanie rushed over to him and they hugged. Ted held the gun for a minute, staring at me with a wary gaze. My charming smile must have won him over. He stuck the gun back in the waistband of his pants.

"Who are you?" Stephanie asked.

"My name is Jarrod Banyon. By profession I'm a private detective. Your parents hired me to find you."

Alarm flashed across her face. "Did you tell them where—"

I shook my head. "No. The last I heard, they think you were going north. I don't plan on telling them anything either, not until I talk to you and Ted. They are also interested in the idol you stole. I assume you did take it."

She nodded. "It was hurting Tiffany. It—"

"They're evil people, Mr. Banyon. You can't tell them where we are," Landers said.

I smiled. He wasn't the first young man who thought his girlfriend's parents were mean. But he may have had more cause for his view than most boyfriends.

"Why don't we sit down?" I suggested.

The two held hands as they stepped down to a pew.

I looked around. A chair was nearby a small table that held a projector for flashing overheads of song lyrics. I grabbed the chair and placed it in front of the couple.

"I browsed through your diary, Ted. It's very interesting reading. A bit unbelievable."

He shook his head. "It might seem that way, but it's not. I

talked about my suspicions with Rev. Tibbets. At first he was cautious, but then too many things fell into place. He reluctantly agreed with me. If you talk to him—"

"Can't do that. He was murdered."

A shocked gasp came from both Ted and Stephanie. The news started Stephanie crying again.

"How? When?"

"By bullet. Yesterday morning. When I arrived at his house to talk to him, someone had shot him. I called the police."

"Oh, no," Stephanie said. She hung her head. The sobs increased in intensity. "He was our only hope..."

Ted put his arm around her.

I reached over and gently touched her hand. "Not your only hope. I'm on your side too, Stephanie."

I was surprised when she squeezed my hand and surprised even more at her strength. "Thank you, Mr. Banyon."

"But I must tell both of you—" I looked at her, then at Ted—"there are other people looking for you. It might be better if you go to the police."

Landers shook his head. "We can't do that, and it's not just because we don't want to. There are other things to consider. If we did that, Stephanie would be in danger."

"I think he's right, Mr. Banyon," Stephanie said. "We didn't get a chance to tell Rev. Tibbets that we were running away, but if he knew the background and circumstances that—"

A glare of headlights flashed against the pulpit. From outside the building, a car's engine sputtered and died.

I looked at the duo. "Expecting anyone?"

A dark flash of fear came from their eyes.

I grabbed my gun. "Is there an exit?" I asked Landers.

He pointed to a side door. "The hall corridor leads to an outside exit."

"You all stay here. I'll check the visitors."

I ran down the corridor and pushed the door. It opened

silently. I crouched down as I stepped onto the grass. Voices came from the front of the church. A car door banged shut.

I edged forward. Clouds roiled overhead. The air had a misty smell in it, a foreshadowing of rain.

Two cars had stopped in the parking lot. One still had its headlights on. Two men walked over to it. One of them could have been the tall man Alma Randolph had described. Two other men got out of the second car.

I moved to the corner of the church. There was no cover between me and the cars, but that worked both ways. There was no cover for them either.

The tall man barked an order to the other three. He was clearly the leader. He must have known about the exit doors. He pointed to his shorter companion and gestured around the church. He made the same motion—for the other side of the church—to a second companion. His shorter companion started walking toward me.

I stepped away from the building. "Don't do it," I shouted. "Stay where you are."

"Who the—"

"You're on private property. You have five seconds to leave."

"You ain't—"

"Four ... "

"Got no—"

"Three..."

"Kill him!" the tall man shouted.

He was wise enough to duck and roll behind a car as he yelled the order. I fired and heard a cry of pain. My bullet plunked into the man behind him, higher than I wanted. Too much shoulder, not enough heart.

I ducked as a whiz of air flew past my ear. A knife chunked into the wall behind me. Shorty was a knifer. He was also quick. He had a second knife in his hands when my two bullets lifted

57

him up and tossed him back. He thumped on the car's hood, then slid into the dirt.

I rolled again as a bullet pinged in the grass beside me. I fired. The bullet banged into the car's fender. Another shot came from the west of the building, from the fourth man. But he didn't have a good angle. His volley soared over my head.

An engine roared from behind. Car lights flashed. Then the Pontiac skidded around a corner. The back wheels gained traction. Dirt spurted out as it headed away. "No!" I yelled.

Foolishly, the tall man raised up to aim at the retreating duo. I fired and heard his moan as my bullet hit its target. Whether to shoot at the car or to help his buddy, the fourth man ran from behind the other corner of the church. I fired twice. Two bloody spots appeared on his shirt. He spun around, then fell like a lump of concrete to the ground.

I needed some more light. I ran to the second car and yanked the headlights on, then flicked on the inside light. My bullet had sliced through the tall man's throat. He gurgled blood. His mouth opened, but no sounds came out. The blood flowed smoothly and quickly over his shirt and onto the asphalt. I had hit the aorta. He was about thirty seconds from hell. I walked over to the wounded man, who was moaning and holding his shoulder. Streams of red flowed between his fingers.

I grabbed the back of his shirt and slammed him against the car. "Let's talk."

"I don't know nothing." He eyed me with a frightened, hostile glare.

"You know who hired you."

"Anders did. I've worked for him before."

"Who is Anders?"

He jerked his head toward the fallen, tall man. "He's right over there."

I jerked the gun barrel under his chin. "If I checked his driver's license, would it have that name?"

He swallowed hard. A drop of spittle came from the trembling lips. "Don't know what his license says. That's the name I know him by."

"What were you supposed to do tonight?"

He hesitated, the smell of fear became stronger.

"Don't antagonize me," I said.

"Grab a girl and take her back to Daytona Beach."

"Just the girl? What about the boy?"

He shook his head. "The boy didn't matter. The girl was to be taken alive."

"So you were going to kill the boy?"

He shrugged. "If it came to that."

"Anything else?"

He turned and spit out some blood. "They had some type of object with them. Anders wanted to take it back with the girl. He said it was very important."

"Did he say why it was important?"

He shook his head. "He didn't say. I didn't ask."

"Who was Anders hired by?"

"He didn't say. I didn't ask."

"Did you also help kill Rev. Roy Tibbets?"

His eyes were blank this time. He looked at me with a puzzled expression.

I backed off, then waved the Glock at him. "Take off."

Keys had been left in the ignition of one of the cars. He slid in the driver's seat and, with his good arm, guided the car out of the complex.

I walked over to Shorty. His second knife had fallen a few inches from his fingers. I didn't doubt that other knives had hit their target. But I recalled the old line about the definition of a fool—a man who brings a knife to a gun fight.

"Do all private detectives have your mordant sense of humor?" Mrs. Canterley had asked.

No. I'm unique. I sighed and flipped open my cell phone. I

59

was about to become acquainted with the Walton County Sheriff's Department. I didn't think local law enforcement was going to be happy with my visit to their fair county.

Ten

I f criminals had to fill out as much red tape as police and prosecutors do, the crime rate would fall drastically. Computers have helped deal with the paper overload, but forests are still being decimated so we can officially keep track of thugs.

The first Walton County deputy who arrived notified the sheriff and, in a short time, there were five patrol cars as well as two ambulances on the Shady Oaks grounds. The sheriff, Sam T. Shifflett, was a stout man of medium height with eyes of burnt coal. Sheriff Sam T. was not happy. He did not like suddenly having three dead bodies in his county. I gathered he wasn't enthusiastic about private detectives either.

I told my story several times, then was asked back to the station whereupon I repeated it again in a small interrogation room to a balding, sleepy-eyed investigator. He carefully jotted down a few comments, but not my full answers. But after he went over my story time and time again, repeating statements I had made, I realized he had a photographic memory. His drowsy manner should have won an Oscar. I began to wonder if I was guilty of something.

The sheriff let me know that the county would provide hospitality for at least one night and named a local motel that wasn't far from the sheriff's department building. He also requested I not leave the county until he gave the OK. I said that was fine. After you have been found in the midst of three dead bodies, you don't want to anger the authorities over small things.

Besides, I supposed I was fortunate to not spend the night in a jail cell. I gathered the department had talked to Detective Owen in Flagler County and he had verified at least some of the details I gave. An overheard part of a conversation informed me that one of the dead men had been identified and had a few felonies on his rap sheet. That might have made the deputies more amenable. At least I got a "good night, sir," when I left the department.

The room was comfortable and spacious. I dipped the little plastic motel cup in the bucket full of ice. I had brought a bottle of bourbon in my suitcase. I poured some liquor over the ice, then added some coca-cola.

"Why do you spoil good bourbon with Coke?" a friend had asked me once.

"It's the way I drink it."

I took a long swig. I didn't want to read any of Ted's papers again. Not tonight. There was an uneasiness in the air, and it prickled my skin. A thousand goose bumps ran up and down my arms and shoulders.

It was the second time that I hoped Pastor Haniford's prayer warriors were not taking the day off.

The next morning, before I had my anticipated session with Walton County law enforcement, I phoned Deke Slattery. Slattery is a former Marine captain who now does detective work, but his specialty is body guarding. He works with a young man named Diego, who handles knives as well as last night's assailant. He also has exceptional skills as a marksman. I doubted Diego's immigration papers were in order, but I wasn't going to be picky.

Unless Slattery had lost weight since the last time I saw him, he filled out his favored beach shirt and slacks at two hundred and sixty-five pounds. Some of the weight had come since his military days but, even now, he was not fat, or slow. His hearty voice jangled the cell phone.

"Jarrod! Hello! Want to set up a golf game?"

"Not today, Deke. I need to hire you. I have a young couple that needs protection."

"Who am I protecting Romeo and Juliet from? Lousy in-laws?" He laughed with such a ferocity it might have busted windows.

"I'm not sure who yet but four people tried to kill them last night."

That calmed his boisterous manner.

"And?"

"Three are dead. One's wounded."

"How did you let that last one get away?"

"There was a lot going on. It was a busy time."

He laughed again. If the previous bellow hadn't broken any windows, the panes were shattering by now.

"I think this is a two-man job," I said.

"I can bring Diego along. The little spic's getting restless."

"You do realize that, nowadays, it is not appropriate to refer to employees as 'spics.' "

"I don't. Not always. Sometimes I call him a wetback."

"Nice to see there's some variety there."

"Besides, he calls me a redneck."

"I see why the partnership works so well."

He laughed. "I think you have sadly incorporated much of the current political zeitgeist into your own thinking, forgetting that the superficial sensitivity of our day is often a mask for hostility and an attack on the First Amendment."

"Yeah, that must be it," I said.

"You may have freedom of speech or you can go through life unoffended, but you can't have both."

I smiled. "Don't get much of a chance to use that degree, do you, Deke?"

"Not here. And the little spic's not impressed with it. By the way, we're thinking of calling our business The Redneck and Spic Agency. Kind of catchy, don't you think?"

"Memorable. I'll say that for it. Is Diego still as good as he was?"

"Can shoot the legs off a fly at two hundred yards."

"Good. I am tracking the couple and can give you more details when I see you. When can you leave?"

"Right now."

I paused. "About sixty miles east of here, at the Marianna exit at State Road 231, there is a restaurant and convenience store. It will take a while to untangle myself from the sheriff's office here. Meet you there at about four."

"That should give us plenty of time."

I crossed the street to a restaurant and ordered bacon and eggs for breakfast. As I sipped the coffee, I wondered about the other option. I could simply reveal to the authorities the whereabouts of the couple and have them taken into protective custody. But Ted and Stephanie had said just enough to make me hesitate. It was also true that I had complete confidence in Deke and Diego.

I had chewed the last piece of toast when I saw the squad car pulled up in the motel parking lot. I figured the balding investigator wanted to go over my story one more time.

When I got back to the motel, forty minutes before checkout time, I phoned the business number of Bolly Canterley. When he answered, I told him his daughter was in great danger. He listened silently as I described the events of the previous night.

"You killed three of them," he said in a voice edging into incredulity.

"Yes. I think they were professionals, but they were not as good as they thought they were. Who would be enemies of your daughter?"

There was a pause on the line. "I don't know. This is shocking, Mr. Banyon. I can't explain it."

"Neither can I. Not yet."

I slapped the phone shut after telling him I'd talk to him again when I returned to Daytona Beach.

Can't explain you either, I thought.

That evening I met Deke and Diego. I sipped a Coke as they rambled in—Deke in his red tropical shirt with green palm trees on it and Diego in a gold T-shirt with a silver chain as a belt on his black slacks, and a gold chain around his neck. On his sizable forearm was a tattoo of a head of a mountain lion, mouth open in a roar. Slattery was three inches taller than his young Hispanic friend and half again as broad. They waved and sat down at the table. I told them the couple had apparently hid out for the night and were above the Florida-Georgia line.

"Want us to make contact with them when they stop?" Slattery asked.

"I leave that to you. You can or just keep them under surveillance. Whatever you think is best," I said.

"How long will you need us?"

"That I don't know,"

I handed them an envelope full of money. It was part of Canterley's advance to me. "That should hold you for about a week."

Slattery grabbed half the bills and gave the other half to his partner. Diego crumpled up the money and stuffed it in his pants pocket.

"We're friends, Jarrod. We'll give you a discount. Fifty percent," Slattery said.

"Hey, we're not that friendly," Diego said. But he flashed a big smile as he spoke. "Ten percent."

I smiled too. "Just keep them safe. Bad things happened to the original Romeo and Juliet. I want these two to survive."

"Anyone tries to take them out, they'd better have an army with them."

"*Sí*," Diego said. "And if they have an army, it's got to be better than the Mexican army."

Deke ordered a beer from a waitress, as did Diego. Then Deke turned toward me. "Do you know what we're up against?"

Diego shrugged. "Does it matter? We stop whoever comes."

"My associate doesn't have much curiosity. I have a much more analytical mind."

I smiled. "I wish I could give you something to be analytical with, but I don't know who our opponents are. All I know is they want to grab the girl and the figurine, and I don't know why."

"The figurine?"

I had forgotten to mention the Aztec dwarf to the pair. I gave them a brief description of the idol.

"Our young couple has it?"

"That's my assumption, unless they ditched in somewhere along the way. If so, the Danielsons are not going to be happy, and they were not the cheeriest couple I've ever met to begin with."

Florida State University was only about fifty miles to the east, so I decided to do a little research before I returned to Daytona. I wondered if even the FSU religion department could provide intelligent answers to my queries. On my way over I phoned Kevin Nadler. His answering machine told me he was probably playing golf or fishing, but if I left my number...I did. I had never met Nadler but knew him by reputation. Several of the current officers in the department highly praised for him for being a thorough, point-by-point investigator with a streak of honesty as wide as the St. Johns River after a massive rain.

The first few people I talked to at FSU were quite helpful. When I told them the type of expertise I needed, they directed me to a Dr. T. Warren Hersfeld in the anthropology department. Dr. Hersfeld also had a degree in religion from the university's football nemesis down in Gainesville. Despite that fact, FSU gave him tenure, which spoke well of Dr. Hersfeld. I was under the impression they blackballed former Gators.

He was a lanky professor, dressed in a regular shirt and slacks. An expertly groomed black and gray goatee gave him a distinguished look. As did the pipe he smoked. He was straight from central casting. He took his pipe from his mouth before answering.

"If I understand you correctly, Mr. Banyon, you want to know if any particular idol from, say the Aztec period, would have special significance for a collector that would make it more valuable than others of the period?"

I nodded. "That pretty well sums it up."

He tapped the stem of his pipe on his lips. "And the reason for the inquiry concerns a violent crime over in Flagler County?"

"Yes. The murder of a missionary. His mission fields were Mexico and Central America. He was back for a vacation when he was killed. I think the stolen artifact is connected with his death."

I reached in my pocket and showed Dr. Hersfeld the now well-worn photograph. "This artifact."

He took the photograph and studied it. There was a small magnifying glass on his desk. He took it and eyed the picture again. "Very, very good condition. Is this an accurate rendition of the object?"

"I assume so. I haven't seen the real thing. I don't know when that was taken, but I believe it's a recent shot."

He hummed and ahhed, then placed the magnifying glass back in its holder. "It's in excellent condition and would bring a good price from people who deal in such items. But I see nothing special about this object. It's a replica of one of the sacrificial gods of the Aztec culture, a fact that would mean little to contemporary dealers or investors." He shrugged. "It might have additional significance if the buyer still practiced some of the older religions but besides that..."

"Why would it be valuable to that particular buyer?"

Dr. Hersfeld smiled. "That was something of a joke, Mr. Banyon. Anthropological humor."

I smiled too. "Humor *me*, professor. If someone, or a group of people, practiced the old religions, why would they want this idol?"

"I'm not sure they would. But some idols are believed by adherents to have special powers. If they can obtain one for a ceremony, then they believe the outcome is virtually assured. Depending on how an idol was used in a pagan culture can make it more dynamic. Adherents believe a great deal of spiritual power can be stored in an idol and released by the right ceremony."

"But all those religions have died out."

"Oh, no, Mr. Banyon. In fact, they are experiencing a revival. There are voodoo rites being practiced in New Orleans and Miami, as well as a few other places. Santeria is another occult religion that has gained popularity with some new immigrants. New York, California, Florida, as well as other areas, have Santeria rituals practiced there."

Then I remembered one of the late Rev. Tibbets' areas of expertise. "How about old-fashioned witchcraft and black magic? Are they experiencing a revival too?"

He nodded. "That's not my field, but some colleagues have told me there is a resurgence of what's called black magic in the land. If so, those practitioners would have a special reverence for specific idols. They would want to use them in rituals."

"Could those ceremonies be held any time?"

He shook his head. "Oh no. Just as Christians or Jews have special holy days, there are special days in the, well, satanic calendar. All Hallows Eve is one."

I must have had a blank look.

"Halloween, Mr. Banyon," Hersfeld said. "Other ceremonies depend on the phases of the moon and planets. Astrology is very important in the older religions."

"In black magic also?"

"Yes."

He handed the picture back to me. I put it in my pocket.

"But such rituals demand a sacrifice, don't they?"

"Santeria and voodoo often use animals such as chickens or goats in their rituals. Blood is a necessary element for any sacrifice."

"Do they use humans sometimes?"

Dr. Hersfeld shifted a bit uneasily in his seat. "Certainly in the past humans have been used, but I don't think—"

"But if we are experiencing a revival of pagan beliefs, wouldn't it be logical to assume that a few devout occultists might try to...go the whole way—a human sacrifice?"

"I think that is entirely speculative, Mr. Banyon."

I got up and thanked him for his time.

It was a Florida day in April—bright, sunny, humid. But there was a chill in the air. I took out the photo of Stephanie and the picture of the idol and looked at both of them. Beauty and ugliness. Light and darkness. Good and evil.

I have my flaws—some of them serious. If I'm riding to the rescue of Stephanie Canterley, then I have no doubt I'm a tarnished knight. But in this eternal struggle, I like to think I'm on the side of the angels—the divine ones, not the fallen ones.

Eleven

Bolly Canterley had shaved his cactus stubble and Geneva Canterley was no longer in a bathrobe when I entered the house. Canterley walked back to his study. I followed and Geneva took up her place behind me. Single file. A bit like two guards escorting a prisoner to the jail, or to the execution chamber. Canterley sat behind his desk. His wife walked over and stood by a bookcase. Neither of them smiled. They looked concerned and irritated, but I wondered if it was Stephanie they were worried about.

Geneva had been without a cigarette for several minutes. It must have taken a toll on her, for she opened a pack and stuck a filter between her lips. She smoked while I told them of my trip to Walton County.

"Have you any guess who would have hired those four men?" I said.

"We certainly don't," Canterley said quickly and gruffly. "We hired you because Ben Murdock stressed your discretion and efficiency. Apparently, those others were not discreet, nor were they efficient."

I thought I detected a note of regret about that last part.

"They didn't expect any opposition," I said. "What bothers me is their ruthlessness. They expected to kill Ted. They wanted Stephanie alive, and they wanted to take the idol, but Ted didn't matter."

I stared at Canterley, but he merely shook his head. "I can't explain that either. This is very puzzling."

"Perhaps the idol is more valuable than we thought," Geneva said. "Someone wants it and doesn't care how they get it."

I looked toward her. "That's possible. But if they only cared about the idol, why not kill both Stephanie and Ted? Or allow both to live. Why worry about one and not the other?"

Geneva didn't answer, just bit into the filter. The cigarette's end flared red. "You certainly did your job, Mr. Banyon. You protected the charming duo."

I wondered if I was getting a bit paranoid. Just like her husband's, Geneva's voice seemed to have a trace of remorse.

"Still, it's a shame you let her get away," Geneva said.

"Gunfire can be a bit distracting. But I found her once. I can find her again."

"Please bring her back when you do," Canterley said. "The last couple of months have been tough with some of the problems we are facing with Stephanie. Young people get like that sometimes, but we want to make things up with her."

His voice held conviction, but it didn't convince me. I was beginning to hold a very jaundiced view of the Canterleys. I looked at him and kept thinking of that diamondback rattler, his tongue flicking out.

"Stephanie wouldn't have any enemies, would she? Any you would know about?"

He shook his head. "She is a popular and friendly girl. No one dislikes her."

Perhaps it was my suspicious glare that caused Canterley to reach into his pocket and bring out the blue checkbook again. He grabbed a pen and clicked it. 'You've had expenses, Mr. Banyon, and I realize this case could have cost you your life. I still want you to find Stepanie and bring her back. And the idol too, of course." He scribbled hastily and handed me the check. "Will another two thousand keep you on the case?"

I took it. "Yes. I will protect her," I said. I didn't say

anything about bringing her back, just protecting her. I think the nuance was lost on Canterley.

"Do you have any idea where she is?" he asked.

"Not right now. I will have to do some more...investigating."

He didn't like the answer but, after a moment, simply shrugged. I stood up and turned to walk out. As I did, I spied a title on the bookcase Geneva Canterley was leaning against. I walked toward it and pulled the book partially from the shelf.

"Do much reading, Mr. Banyon?" Geneva asked.

"Actually, I do. Although I grew up in the media age I've always enjoyed the printed word." I tapped the book. "I saw this book over at the Danielsons. You must have similar interests." I pushed *Ancient Altars* back into the stack.

Geneva gave me her cold-eyed stare. "We are both interested in ancient religions. Perhaps that explains part of Stephanie's behavior. Some teenagers rebel and leave their faith. Since we are not Christians, Stephanie might have embraced it just to irritate us. We always felt a faith that emphasizes forgiveness and mercy is for cowards."

"Do what thou will shall be the whole of the law?"

Geneva's eyes widened with surprise. Then she nodded. "Yes. It's better than turning the other cheek and letting people rob you blind. Why should anyone follow a faith whose founder died on a cross?"

"Christians believe he was resurrected."

"But why die at all when you can rule?"

"Why serve in heaven when you can rule in hell?"

"Precisely. So you've read Milton? Wasn't Satan a rather strong and dynamic figure in the poem? God seems rather weak and pedantic."

I shrugged. "I wasn't impressed by the fallen angel. Even if you rule in hell, it's still hell."

Her cigarette burned down to the hilt. It had a pungent,

tangy smell. I wondered what she was smoking. "Are you a member of your husband's hunt club, Mrs. Canterley?"

"I go out occasionally. Why do you ask?"

I looked at her. "You have a certainly ruthlessness, and the intense focus of a predator."

She sniffed and ground the cigarette out in an ashtray. "I will take that as a compliment, Mr. Banyon, whether it was meant as one or not."

"Stephanie didn't inherit that trait, did she?"

She looked amused and gave a curt laugh. "No, she didn't. Which is why life will be tough for her."

They didn't bother to walk me to the door. I didn't mind.

I decided I needed a brief break. However, the schedule would not allow a trip to the Bahamas. So I drove out to the Coastal Isles gym. After a vigorous sixty-minute workout, I showered, then slipped into the club's hot tub. The hot water ripples eased muscles and tensions. Solitude and hot, swirling water help you think. Wasn't it Alchimedes who experienced a scientific revelation in his bath? I, unlike the Greek scientist, received no sudden bolts of insight. I could not piece the events of the past days together in any coherent, recognizable mosaic. After thirty minutes, I climbed out, dripping water. Refreshed, but no wiser.

I returned to my office, where there was a message from Kevin Nadler on my machine. I called him back and told him of my interest in one of his cases. He had a pleasant voice and a pleasant personality. He said he was coming into the city later in

74

the day and could drop by my office. I thanked him.

I shouted "come in" when I heard the soft, timid knock on the door and was surprised when Tiffany Danielson opened it. "Mr. Banyon?"

"Come in."

She walked forward. Beside her, holding her hand, came a high school linebacker. He was distinctive not just for his size but for his old-fashioned hairstyle—a blond crewcut. Round nose but a square jaw and a wide smile. He projected friendliness, but I'm sure he was intimidating to those on the other side of the football.

"I just wanted to ask about Stephanie. Have you found her?"

"Yes and no. I found her, but she's missing again."

She looked puzzled. I pointed to two chairs in the office and asked them to sit down. When they did, I told them that Stephanie and Ted were involved in something dangerous and detailed the Shady Oaks gun battle.

Tiffany groaned and shook her head. "This is terrible."

"Not as bad as it could have been," I said. "They could both be dead by now."

"Are you...are you still going to try and find them again?"

I nodded. She looked so devastated I wanted to comfort her. "Let's say I have a few leads. But it might be good for them to find a safe place and stay there for a while, until I get this sorted out."

She nodded. She unhooked her hand and stuck it in her purse, then brought out a Kleenex and wiped her tears. "Thank you for saving them, Mr. Banyon." She shook herself, as if clearing all thoughts. She looked toward her friend. "I'm sorry. I haven't introduced you two. Mr. Banyon, this is Frank Averill."

When I offered my hand, he crunched it in his huge paw. I grimaced. "Play football by any chance?"

He nodded. "Got to the high school state championships last year. Hope to do as well at college. I have a scholarship to

Central Florida."

"A good team. Good school."

"I want to thank you too, Mr. Banyon. Tiffany told me what happened the first time you met her. The incident with her father. If he tries that again, he'll answer to me."

"Frank—"

"No one hits you," he said ominously. "No one."

Chivalry wasn't dead after all. If he had been old enough to drink, I would have offered him one. I smiled. He returned it. There was an immediate understanding between us. Here was another knight, perhaps an untarnished one. I saw in his eyes and manner his complete dedication to Tiffany.

"Since you're here, I'd like to ask you something. What can you tell me about Stephanie's relationship with her parents? Her parents are unlike any others ..." I let the sentence drop.

Tiffany nodded. "They've always been odd...and distant. I think that's the word for it. *Distant*. Aloof. As if in another dimension. That's one thing Stephanie and I had in common. We've been friends since the age of six. My parents are in their own little space too. Both Stephanie and I realized that we were ...isolated, I guess. We would never truly fit in with our families. We lived in the same house with our folks, but it was never really a home. Our parents were more like custodians...or guards. But the latter gives the impression our home life was harsh or cruel, and that's not really the case. More like indifferent."

"Still, most parents might be outraged when a boy takes their daughter and runs away even, as in this case, when the daughter left voluntarily," I said.

Tiffany looked uneasy. She wriggled in the chair. "Well...there's...I'm not sure I should talk about it. I don't think it has any bearing on finding her..."

When her words trailed off, I said, "I'd like to know everything I can about her. It might help me connect some very

76

loose ends."

Tiffany sighed, then smiled. "Mr. Banyon, Stephanie and I shared something else. It really brought us closer together and cemented our friendship in junior high and later. It's...it's..."

"I've heard about everything. You don't have to be hesitant."

She gave a ring of sharp laughter. It seemed to break the tension. "You may not have heard this. Know anything about neuters, Mr. Banyon?"

I shrugged. I hadn't heard the word for a while. "People who have little or no sexual drive?"

She nodded. "Gays represent about 2 to 3 percent of the population. It's estimated neuters are also about 2 to 3 percent. They get a lot less publicity, though."

I recalled what Meadows said about Tiffany turning down his son, and others, for dates. "So you and Stephanie..."

She nodded. "All the sexual buzz and activity by our classmates was a mystery to us, until recently. We felt no attraction for men...or women for that matter. We were very happy most of the time—or at least I was when the depression lifted—but we had no sexual desire at all. In fact, it was more than that. When we even thought of the sexual act, we both were repulsed, to the point of being almost physically sick."

I looked at Averill, then glanced back at Tiffany. "You said until recently."

"Five months ago I began attending Souls Harbor. A short time later I was born again, and baptized in the Holy Spirit. I didn't change at that moment, but gradually I began to feel... some rather odd urges. They kept increasing, and then I realized what they were. The human sexual drive." She smiled. "It's rather wonderful."

"It can be inconvenient at times too."

"Yes. I'm finding that out. I was always baffled about children too. I never desired any. But now I find myself looking very fondly on babies and toddlers. They are so cute."

"But they need good parents."

She nodded. "I didn't say anything to Stephanie, even after she was born again. Then gradually I broached the subject and realized the same thing had happened to her. Sexual affections had been awakened. She liked Ted before conversion—he was so sweet and nice—and he went with her even though he knew there was no attraction and no chance of sex. He...he fell in love with her."

I nodded.

"I think both sets of parents knew of our condition, although neither one of us talked about it. We didn't talk about much at all with our parents. Frankly, I don't think the Canterleys care if Stephanie is a virgin or if she's slept with the football squad and saved a day for the baseball jocks. But if they knew she was a neuter, that might explain some things..."

Yes. Perhaps.

Then again, they might care very much if she's a virgin, but not for the traditional reason.

"Thank you, Tiffany. Your information might help the case."

Both stood up and Tiffany offered her hand. "If there's anything we can do to help, Mr. Banyon..."

I nodded. I shook her hand and let her boyfriend crush my fingers again too.

After Tiffany and Frank left, I eased back in my chair, opened the bottom drawer and stuck my foot on it. It's a comfortable position that's conducive to thinking, and sometimes to dozing off. But I was wide awake today. There were far too many dots in this case and I could not connect them. Big red dots, smaller blue ones, and sort of square-shaped green ones. They all went together somehow...I closed my eyes. When I was just about to draw a line between a blue circle and a green square, the phone rang. I didn't recognize the number. When I picked up the receiver it was Pastor Haniford. His voice was frantic.

"Mr. Banyon. I need your advice. I think the church made a huge mistake yesterday."

"What happened?"

"A man called our youth pastor, Scott Tidlow. He said he was from the First Fellowship Church from down south in the county. It's a rather large congregation. He said some members were looking for a retreat for a weekend of solitude and study. He said he was told some of our church youth went to a retreat last summer and he wondered what location it was. Scott told him."

"Of the facility in Walton County?"

"Yes," said Haniford's surprised tone. "How did you know?"

"Never mind. Go on with your story."

"Then the man asked if Ted and Stephanie had been among the youth on the trip. Scott said he thought so. For some reason, the call kept nagging at Scott so he called First Fellowship and asked about it. The pastor said no one down there had called. That they used other facilities for any get-togethers."

"It's okay, Pastor. Ted and Stephanie were there, but they have left."

"Are they safe?"

"Yes."

I told the pastor what happened to the caller and two of his friends. For a long time, the only sound I heard on the line was the pastor's anxious breathing.

"I hope the intercessors haven't quit, Pastor."

He sighed. "We will not quit until Ted and Stephanie are back safe and sound."

"Glad to hear it. By the way, you told me once the late Rev.

Tibbets knew a great deal about demonology."

"Yes, he had seen a number of demonic manifestations. Several times local witch doctors tried to put a curse on him and did other things to try to harass and obstruct his ministry."

"Do you know anyone else who might have a little knowledge of the subject? I think it might have a bearing on this case."

He thought for a moment. "St. John Oberjan. He pastors a church up in Jacksonville. St. John is Haitian and came out of a voodoo cult. He could probably answer any question you have."

I jotted down name and number. I thought I had connected a couple of dots. St. John might be able to tell me if I was right.

Twelve

When the door opened I was expecting retired Detective Nadler, but it was an active detective who walked in. Webb Owen sauntered through the office as if he owned the place, but he smiled and nodded as he pulled up a chair.

'Make yourself at home," I told him.

He crossed his legs, unbuttoned his jacket, then pulled out a cigarette pack. "Mind if I smoke?"

"It's a dying habit."

He grinned. "That's what my wife keeps telling me. She doesn't like me puffing." He stuck a cigarette in his mouth and lit it, then exhaled a cloud of menthol. "I've cut down, but I haven't been able to quit." He turned his law-enforcement laser stare on me. "You have any vices, Banyon?"

"A couple. None that are illegal."

"You know, a few of my colleagues in the sheriff's department here did speak highly of you. They also said you really do have a lousy golf swing."

"I have a bad slice when I get out of rhythm, but I'm working on it."

"Detective Steve Hamilton said you brought in evidence a couple of years ago that helped them nail a murder suspect."

"I do my best to maintain law and order."

Owen seemed to stiffen in the chair. "But you misplaced the young, runaway couple?"

"I wouldn't say misplaced. I was busy and they ran out the

back way."

"You didn't know any of the assailants?"

I shook my head. "Never saw them before. I'm guessing they'd been through the court system a few times, perhaps more than a few."

He nodded and pulled out his reporter's notebook and flipped it open. I grabbed a blue ashtray and moved it to the edge of the desk so it was within Owen's reach. He tapped some ashes in it.

"Two of the three had drug and assault charges against them. One had already done time. Three years in Railford."

"And the other?"

Owen looked at his notebook. "The other was a tall man named Anders Martinez. He has been involved in a variety of activities. A few of them were actually legal. He had an American and Mexican passport and traveled between the two countries."

"So do twelve million other people, but without passports."

Owen thumbed a page in the notebook. "Did the late Mr. Martinez look like an anthropologist to you?"

"That was my second choice of profession for him. Second-rate thug was my first choice."

He nodded. "On his trips to Mexico, Mr. Martinez popped up at excavation sites and digs. From time to time, he obtained a valuable historical item that he sold to the Sea Island Galleries."

This time I stiffened. I eased my chair closer to the desk. "Do tell."

"It is rumored that he did not always come into possession of these items in a legitimate manner. When we asked a Mr. Gary Danielson about this, he said he had not seen Martinez for several months and was unaware the man was in the area."

I gave a sour grin. "Well, that settles it. Danielson's word is gold. Anything else unusual about Martinez?"

Owen flipped the notebook shut. "A minor item. He had a

rather odd tattoo on his chest."

"Let me guess. A heart with the word *Mother*?"

A deep snort of laughter came from the detective. "Hardly. It was a picture of the man with the horns, red eyes and grinning."

"By horns, I assume it wasn't a tattoo of a trumpet player."

"No."

"He had a tattoo of Satan?"

"Good size one too."

"Now he knows if it was a good likeness."

As Owen slipped his notebook back in his pocket, he stared at me again. "You're not holding anything back from me, are you, Mr. Banyon?"

"If I knew who killed Tibbets or who sent those four thugs or about Ted and Stephanie—or had any clue—I'd tell you. I want the young couple alive and whoever killed the reverend dead or behind bars."

It wasn't a complete answer to his question but, after a few seconds in silence, it seemed to satisfy him. "See you around," he said as he walked out of the office.

Owen's visit made me question if I had made the right judgment. So I called Deke and Diego. Deke reported the fleeing couple was currently in southwest Georgia heading north on state road 19. The town they seemed to be approaching was Americus, a small farming community. He had seen nothing suspicious.

As I dropped the cell phone in its case, my office phone rang again. Suddenly I was getting more traffic than Grand Central Station. When I answered it, I heard Pastor Haniford's voice.

"Mr. Banyon, there is something here I think you'd want to see. Our mail was just delivered. There was a small package addressed to the church, but it also had your name on it." He paused for a minute. "I think it's the idol you were looking for."

"I'll be right down," I said.

I phoned Nadler and, again, got a recording. We had not managed to talk to each other directly yet. I explained I had been called away suddenly but would be back in the office at four. I apologized for any inconvenience and emphasized I still wanted very much to speak to him. Then I said, if he came in at five, I'd buy him a drink at a bar around the corner.

On the way down to Souls Harbor, I phoned the Sea Island Galleries. The man who answered had a deep, raspy voice that sounded like he was just a few points shy of the heart failure red zone. When I asked about the Danielsons, he said they'd be away for several days.

"May I ask who this is?" he said, practically wheezing into the phone.

I said I was a private investigator known to the Danielsons. I told him I might have found the missing artifact.

"Yes, they mentioned you might be calling. They should be back in the store Friday evening."

I thanked him.

Fifteen minutes later I pulled into the parking lot of Souls Harbor. When I entered the church, the secretary said the pastor was expecting me. I walked down the corridor. His office door was open.

For a few seconds, I stood in his office doorway and stared at the black figure. It sat on his desk. It was even uglier than its picture. The sacrificial knife glistened in the light. Even though the figure was made six hundred years ago, the sharpened teeth—ready for the victims—had not dulled. It had seen thousands—perhaps tens of thousands—of human hearts ripped out and offered in ghastly rituals. Tens of thousands died, but it remained. The black eyes of death stared into space.

Pastor Haniford came and stood beside me. "This is an evil object, Mr. Banyon. No Christian should have it in his house or office. No one should, for that matter."

I didn't disagree. I reached for it and picked it up. It was so heavy I almost dropped it. I guessed it weighed twenty compact pounds or more. Six hundred years ago it was on an altar of death. Six hundred years later, its lethal influence was still getting people killed.

"Why did Stephanie send it to you, Pastor?"

"She didn't want to carry it with her, which I can understand, but she also didn't want to give it back to the Danielsons. She believed this is what caused Tiffany Danielson's depression, and so do I."

I showed him a baffled expression.

He didn't backtrack a bit. "That may sound strange to you, Mr. Banyon, and even unbelievable. But Rev. Tibbets could have told you there are objects that can attract demonic spirits and some of those entities can be spirits of depression or oppression."

He walked around behind his desk and sat down. I sat in a chair. The black object was between us. The idol was horrifying but, even so, I had difficulty taking my gaze off it.

"I had a member some years ago who had an Indian heritage. He came to me one day and told me that, for several weeks, he and his wife were experiencing severe oppression. He couldn't figure it out. It was morning and evening, day and night. There was nothing in the natural world to explain it. Until that time they were very happily married, their finances were solid, they had no physical or emotional problems. In fact, they enjoyed every day. But the oppression was just like a gray cloud around them."

I finally shook my gaze from the hideous little man and

looked at the pastor, although I didn't see how his story would help me solve the case.

"I went over to their residence and walked through the house praying. I think the Lord led me to one particular object, a painting showing a Native American dance. But the dance was in praise of one of the Indian gods, which was demonic. The spirits that they worshiped was not the Holy Spirit. I looked at the painting and knew there was something wrong, spiritually, with it. Fortunately, the couple listened to me. They took the painting out in their back yard and burned it, then repented and asked for the blood of Jesus to cleanse them from any unrighteousness."

"And?"

"That ended the oppression. They've never had any trouble with it since. I know of several other pastors who could tell you similar stories. Sometimes we don't understand how or why an object acts like a demonic magnet. We just know some objects do." He pointed to the idol. "This little creature has a strong demonic influence." He looked at me. "I realize this is difficult for you to believe, Mr. Banyon."

"Maybe not as difficult as it would have been three days ago," I told him. "Let's say I'm skeptical but open to...new ideas."

He smiled.

"But why wouldn't this cause depression to the parents, as well as Tiffany?"

"There is a different reaction from Christians and non-Christians." He cleared his throat. "This is something else that's difficult to explain."

"I have a Baptist background if that makes it easier."

"Well, let's just say in that household, Tiffany was born-again and, thus, the enemy of this creature and all he represents. If you were an entity around this thing, who would attack? Your enemies, or your allies?"

I was thinking about his statement when he asked about Ted and Stephanie. Usually, I like to play the cards close to my chest. I'm not one to share confidences. So I wasn't sure quite why, but I told the pastor I had the two under surveillance. The last I heard the couple was on their way toward Americus, I said.

"Now that you mentioned Americus, I think I recall Ted saying he had relatives in Georgia, on his mother's side. We were talking once, and he said his family would visit up there almost every summer when he was a child. His relatives had a farm nearby. Grew...er...what was it? Watermelons, I think, in addition to other crops."

"If that's true, then they might have a safe haven. I would like to keep them out of harm's way for a while."

"You haven't told this to Stephanie's parents?"

I explained I didn't particularly trust the Canterleys. If you could shrink them down to their basic components, they might look like the little black figure on his desk.

Haniford chuckled. "But you're still on the case?"

I nodded. "When I first met Tiffany she compared Ted and Stephanie with Romeo and Juliet, but then she remembered that play was a tragedy. I just don't want this case to end the same way. I also promised Tiffany I'd help her friends."

"Very admirable, Mr. Banyon."

"I'm not sure about that. But I don't like to quit in the middle of a case either." I looked at the black figure again. "So what are you going to do with the little Aztec?"

"If it was up to me, I'd burn it," Haniford said. "But it's stolen property. I have no legal right to it. Would the police be interested in it?"

I shook my head. "I don't think so. I don't think the Danielsons ever filed a complaint report, so I doubt the police would care...the Danielsons, would, though."

He looked at me. "I hate to say this, but perhaps you'd like to take it back to them, although I'd like to take a hammer to it. Nothing good can come from this ungodly creation. I have applied the blood of Jesus to it, so that will stop any demonic manifestations."

"Good," I said.

I wasn't being sarcastic, nor did I have a patronizing smile this time. With everything else that had been going on, demonic manifestations were the last thing I needed.

But one thing puzzled me. I had read most of Ted's diary and he, like the pastor, was convinced the idol was dangerous. So why send it back? I know Christians don't believe in theft, but this was pushing honesty to a lunatic extreme. You can't win battles when your opponents lie, cheat, steal, and murder while you maintain the high ethical road.

I told the pastor the Danielsons wouldn't be back in the city for two days and asked if he could keep the object until them. For some reason, I figured the church might be the best place to keep it.

"You can pick it up when you're ready," he said.

Thirteen

I finally got a chance to talk to Kevin Nadler. He buzzed me as I drove back to Daytona Beach. He was currently tied up but wondered if that bar close to my office stayed open late. I told him it did. He said he could drop by for a drink around eight but asked about the subject of the meeting. I said eight would be fine and mentioned the names of Gary and Carmen Danielson From what Raymond had said, the case had been a long time ago so I wondered if Nadler would remember. But he responded immediately.

"Yes, I remember the couple. Sea Island Galleries. Right?"

I said it was.

"See you tonight, Banyon."

There were two Chad Atkinsons in the Daytona Beach-Volusia County phonebook, which was a relief. I thought there might be a half-dozen or so. I pulled out a phonebook that was five years old and checked the listings. The Chad Atkinson on Melody Avenue was listed in the old one too. Unless the Chad Atkinson on Bluebird Lane had moved in recently—which was possible—he should be the younger one. I phoned but got an answering machine saying he was unavailable. Calling up MapQuest on my computer, I discovered Bluebird Lane was a fifteen-minute drive. I decided to say hello.

In fourteen minutes, I wondered if I might be mistaken. Perhaps this Chad Atkinson was a middle-aged businessman who had moved to the city recently. Bluebird Lane was one of the streets in the Harmony Subdivision, a complex of about fifty houses with a recreational hall and tennis courts. It looked like a place for a married man instead of a young bachelor. Although the golf course looked nice.

The Atkinson address was a two-story house trimmed in blue. The two-car garage had only one car in it, a shiny new Camaro. I pulled up into the driveway, noticing the neatly trimmed grass and hedges. When I knocked on the door, there was no answer. After I knocked again, I twisted the doorknob. It wasn't locked. I opened it and peered inside.

"Mr. Atkinson," I said.

It's not superstition to say some rooms or houses have an aura about them. I know one lovely couple who has been married thirty-seven years. Both are vivacious and outgoing. When you walk into their home, there is a lightness—even a beauty—in the air. I have also been in places where the air has been filled with tension. Or places in the forest where, for some reason, my hair began to stand on end. There was nothing by way of nose or eyes or ears to account for that sensation. But something caused the body to tense.

The stillness in the Atkinson house was akin to a red warning signal. I drew my gun and walked in.

"Mr. Atkinson," I said again, in a louder tone this time.

I thought the design was odd. As soon as I opened the door, there were two steps leading up to the living room and, besides them, steps heading down to the basement. I eased up the landing. As I turned left I saw why Atkinson wasn't answering. Several pieces of furniture, including a coffee table, had been overturned. Bloodied and mutilated, Atkinson lay facedown on the carpet, dead.

Only bits and pieces of clothing were on the body. Most of

his back was visible but covered with ugly, red scars, as if a violent animal had clawed him. I turned him over. Two more long, jagged bite or claw marks lined his face. Alive, Atkinson had probably been about six-two, with dark black hair and ebony eyes. A muscular chest and arms showed benefits of regular gym workouts. But he hadn't been strong enough to stop whatever mauled him.

I looked around but the house was quiet. Besides the living room furniture, nothing else seemed to have been disturbed. A glass sat on the kitchen table, as did a small table decoration. The four chairs surrounding the table were in their proper places. A bookcase at the far end of the room had been left undisturbed. As I skimmed his reading material, one title caught my eye. I didn't have time for study, though. I punched the sheriff's department number on my cell phone.

This was the second time in three days that I had found someone murdered. I wondered if I should find another profession.

The police were actually much nicer than I expected. After all, if you are in law enforcement and receive calls from a single individual reporting two murders within three days, you might be tempted to arrest him as a public nuisance, or worse. I did advise the stout gray-haired detective that he might want to call Webb Owen of the Flagler County department because there was a possibility that this crime was linked to a murder up there.

He nodded. "I know Webb. He's a good man."

I decided not to mention the three dead men up in Walton County. Discretion is the better part of valor. As yet, I couldn't explain any of the homicides. I arrived at the Bay Inlet bar about ten minutes to eight. I needed the drink I ordered.

Fourteen

When a tall, gray-haired man walked in the bar, I figured he was former detective Kevin Nadler. If, that is, any policeman or detective is ever former. He looked distinctive, even though he was dressed in a yellow sports shirt and dark slacks, as if ready for a round of golf. But there is one trait I have found common among good detectives. Alert, curious eyes. Often staring out from a very ordinary face. Or a stern, ugly one. Or even a chubby one, with jowls bouncing as they question you. But the eyes are always alert.

They have seen the hideous underside of life—all the emotional wreckage done when humans display the seven deadly sins. But they and their firefighter companions have also seen firsthand—and have demonstrated—the astonishing sacrificial courage of the human race. I saw a poll not too long ago of people who were asked if they had their dream jobs. Most people said no, but most policemen and firefighters said yes. They are the everyday heroes of our civilization.

Nadler trained his alert gaze on me. He had a big, friendly smile and radiated confidence and charisma. I shook his hand.

"Good to finally met you," he said as he took a chair.

I waved to the waitress and asked Nadler what he wanted.

"Beer," he told the waitress.

I waited until Nadler was served and took a sip from his mug before asking my questions.

"I appreciate you coming," I said.

He smiled. "Well, I'm retired. I have a lot of time on my

hands, although I must admit I am pursuing golf with a renewed interest. I have managed to shave five strokes off my handicap. Twelve more and I'll be shooting par."

"A noble goal."

"I think so. But what can I do for you, Mr. Banyon? You didn't ask me here to talk about golf."

"I wish I had. It's a much more pleasant subject. But I wanted to ask you about one of your old cases that involved the Danielsons."

He grunted. "Why would you be interested in that?"

"I don't know if I will be, but I'm on a case now that involves them. A young runaway may have taken one of their artifacts. She sent it back, or at least she sent it to a friend, so soon they will have their property back. I just wanted to gather information about them because the case is taking some odd paths."

Nadler took a large swig of his drink, then placed the mug back on the table. "Back about a decade ago, they were suspects...well, that's not really accurate...they were questioned about a young Mexican man who disappeared and later turned up dead."

"He had business with the Danielsons?"

"He might have had. When we found the body, there was a receipt from a restaurant not far from the Danielsons' business. We asked around a bit and two people said they had seen a young Hispanic man, unshaved and looking grubby, hanging around on the street. He carried a black bag with him. One said she saw him go into the gallery. When we asked Mr. Danielson about it, he said a smelly stranger came into his office and wanted to sell him an antique. He looked at it but said it was not of the quality or type he wanted, so he refused. The man left and that was the end of it."

"But the seller later turned up dead?"

Nadler took another sip of his beer. "Yes, in the western

part of the county, near the Marion County line."

"Anything to connect the Danielsons with the dead body?"

"Nothing directly." He eased forward in his chair and put his arms on the table. "However, I wasn't satisfied with what Gary Danielson told me. Nothing I could put my finger on, mind you, just a little nibbling at the back of the mind. And a hunch that said if you hooked this guy up to a polygraph, there'd be wavy lines all over the place."

I nodded. "That was my impression of him."

"I nosed around and found out that a few days after the dead body was discovered, the Sea Island Gallery had a new South American artifact, larger than most of their other items. It was about two feet tall." He looked at me. "Ever seen their shop?"

"Seen a few items of their inventory. Really ugly stuff."

He smiled. "Ugly stuff that people will pay big money for. That shows you the buyers have too much money."

"And no artistic sense," I said.

I ordered him another beer after he drained his glass. He wiped his mouth with a napkin. "However, when I asked, Mr. Danielson had all the proper papers and even had the name of a store in Mexico where he had allegedly purchased it."

"Did you check that?"

He nodded. "I phoned down and the manager said he dealt in antiques and had done business with the Danielsons before. He even praised them for being such honest brokers."

"That's something suspicious right there."

He laughed as the waitress placed the second beer down on the table. "We had other cases back then and couldn't pursue the murder of an illegal immigrant when we had nothing to go on. We shoved it into the unsolved file." He paused. "Odd thing, though. About six months later, due to latent curiosity, I phoned the Mexican store again. Number had been disconnected. Did a little checking with some Mexican counterparts. Discovered if there had been a store, it had been open for about a week, then

94

shut down and the manager went elsewhere."

"Talk to the Danielsons again?"

He shook his head. "Not with what I had. Shops open and close all the time. There's a lot of dealers—or owners—of antiques. They move around, find something else, no way to prove anything. I had suspicions, but that was all."

I drained my glass and ordered another drink. The waitress was kind enough to bring us a bowl of peanuts. I grabbed a few and ate them. "So it was a dead end?"

Nadler nodded.

I washed a few more peanuts down with my second sour. "By the way, how was the seller killed? I assume it was foul play."

Nadler reached over, took one peanut, and slowly brought it back to his lips. As he chewed he said, "That's the odd thing about it. The man looked like he had been mauled by some type of animal, but the wounds matched nothing that our lab boys had even seen. Not a panther, not a bear, nothing we could match. I didn't like—or trust—the Danielsons, but there was nothing to tie them to the death."

It had been a long day. When the detective walked in, I had been getting drowsy. His words hit me like a splash of ice water. And caused all organs to go on high alert.

"His death was so curious I questioned the coroner about it. He was puzzled. He told me a lot of the markings were not fatal. The lethal blow was a slash to the throat. But Dr. Templeton said—and he admitted this was only a guess—that whatever killed the man didn't kill him quickly. It played with him for a while, like a cat plays with a mouse."

I said nothing but took another sip from my drink.

Nadler raised a finger. "I don't know if this would interest you or not, but the parcel where the body was found belonged to a friend of the Danielsons. The couple is in real estate and some years ago bought more than a hundred acres in west Volusia. I think some of their property winds over into Marion County too. Might be good hunting out there."

"Would the name of the owners be Canterley?"

He nodded.

Fifteen

A day later, after I confirmed that the Danielsons were back in town, I packed the idol in foam and placed it in a satchel.

Gary Danielson looked subdued when I entered Sea Island Galleries. The last time I saw Danielson he had been pawing the ground like a bull ready to charge. Now he looked liked he'd been gelded. The ferocity in his manner had drained away. The intensity of his glare was gone and replaced by a blank, almost indifferent look. Carmen Danielson, though, had clearly gone through the caffeinated beverages. Her round eyes were excited but wary. The smile wasn't friendly.

I was surprised to see the Canterleys also standing quietly in the room, although both looked intently at me and at the package I carried.

"Well, the gang's all here," I said.

"We felt it was our responsibility that our friends lost the idol. We wanted to make sure it was OK," Canterley said.

I held up the satchel I carried. "Safe and sound."

Carmen Danielson nodded. "Please come into the office, Mr. Banyon."

I followed her away from the display tables and down a small hall. I placed the satchel on a desk and opened it. The Danielsons tore away the foam to look at the figure. When they saw it, they smiled. So did the Canterleys.

"Yes," Carmen said. "It's not damaged."

"If it had been, we would have—"

"Gary," Carmen said sharply.

Geneva Canterley looked more intently at the object and fingered it. Her hand caressed the idol as fingers checked the nooks and crevices on the black figure.

"I thought they might try to destroy it," she said.

"Why would they do that?" I said.

The question seemed to shock her, then she smiled. "Well, who knows what teenagers will do nowadays."

"Who knows what adults will do nowadays," I said.

Carmen Danielson gave a frown of annoyance. "Thank you, Mr. Banyon, for bringing back our property. Where did you find it?"

"The couple sent it to their pastor. Perhaps, since they're Christians, they had a guilty conscience about stealing it. The pastor called me. He didn't want to keep it because it wasn't his."

Her lips moved but didn't form a smile. It was a smirk. "We rarely see such honesty nowadays." She looked toward her husband. "We will have to send him a thank-you note."

Her husband nodded. "Tell him how much we appreciate it," he said with only a trace of sarcasm.

I walked to the edge of the table and looked at the idol. "Ugly little thing. If you're going to worship a god, why not worship a handsome god? Why bow down to ugliness and filth?"

Geneva Canterley gave a curt, condescending smile. "Ugliness, like beauty, Mr. Banyon, is in the eye of the beholder."

"I think most beholders would say this little thing ran through an ugly forest and hit every tree." I glanced at Gary Danielson, then pointed at the idol. "You know, there is a resemblance."

She gave a bitter laugh. Danielson didn't. He glared at me with a menacing scowl. "If you want to keep those teeth, Banyon..."

"Gary, shut up. Mr. Banyon would twist you in two," his

98

wife said, then looked at me. "Wouldn't you?"

"I probably could take him."

Danielson fumed. Smoke almost poured from his nose and ears. He pawed the ground again, but said nothing.

Canterley cleared his throat, and the other three immediately looked toward him. It was clear who the leader of the little group was. He walked up to me. "Thank you for recovering the item. It was well worth the money. Please continue to look for Stephanie too."

"I will," I said. I looked over the group. "By the way, Chad Atkinson is dead."

None of them looked all that surprised or even looked like they cared.

Geneva Canterley shrugged. "He dated Stephanie some time ago, but we didn't know all that much about him."

"I thought he might have been friends with you and with this group."

"Why would you think that?"

"You have an interest in the same type of reading material." When her eyebrows shot up, I knew I had hit home. "Both of you have rather esoteric tastes, so I thought you were members of the same club, so to speak." I paused to allow the words to have their effect. "Especially since one of his books is inscribed."

She rolled her tongue in her mouth, then ran it along her lower lip.

"The second time I came to your house, I glanced at the bookcase in your living room. One book was titled *Ancient Altars*. It has chapters on witchcraft and black magic."

I reached in my jacket to lift out a thin cigar. I tore the plastic and slid it out of the clear wrapper. "Mr. Atkinson had a similar volume in his library. It appeared to be well-read. Do you remember what you wrote in it, Mrs. Canterley?"

She waited a moment before answering. "I think I do remember inscribing his book. It was some time ago. But he drifted away after he broke up with Stephanie. We shared an interest in the older religions, a fascination with the past." She shrugged. "After he stopped seeing Stephanie he...lost interest, I guess."

Her husband interrupted. "I don't see what this has to do with anything. We're interested in Stephanie, not Chad Atkinson...although I regret he's dead."

Geneva walked closer to me. As I put the cigar in my mouth she surprised me by bringing out her red lighter and flicking it. She moved it to light the end of my cigar.

"You have sharp eyes, Mr. Banyon, and an alert mind."

"Endless curiosity too," I said. Puffs of smoke came from the cigar.

"Curiosity, Mr. Banyon, killed the cat. It has also contributed to the demise of any number of humans."

She still held the lighter. When she snapped it shut, the click sounded like the clang of cymbals in the silent room.

Sixteen

I decided to take a morning off to think. I wanted to read Ted's diary again, but I thought I would give that a day's rest too. The beach wasn't too crowded. I watched lovely ladies in bikinis walk through the sand and splash in the waves. It was a perfect day for Florida. The sun spread a shiny, golden blanket on the land. The rays reflected off the blue waves. Flecks of gold sparkled on the sand as the light hit a tiny residue of metal or plastic.

A tall, dark-haired lady in a dark blue bikini passed me, warming me with her bright smile. The women seem to get better every year. I didn't like the crudity and the vulgarity on the college holidays, a meat-market of flesh where more than one predator lurks. Never liked the tattoos either. If you have a beautiful body, and loads of these fair ladies did, don't besmirch it with ugliness.

A fair bathing beauty with wind-blown blond hair stopped to make conversation. As she edged closer to me on the sand, she implied she was available for a drink, and more. I politely declined.

I had hoped the brightness would dissipate the events of the past few days. There was a darkness there. I had walked through a door to a different dimension. A dimension, as Rod Serling might say, of grays and shadows, of darkness and blood, of a previously unknown world that had become all too real. Now my world of sun and beach and good liquor and bikinis could never be the same.

I wanted my old world, the world where I was very content before riding out to see Bolly Canterley. And before agreeing to find his daughter and recover the hideous idol for the Danielsons. I wondered if I could ever get it back. I yearned for it the way an old man seeks his lost youth.

I jogged two miles down the beach and two miles back before grabbing a towel and returning to my apartment. After showering, I returned to Ted's diary, with the quaint hope that perhaps I had overreacted the first time I read it. But the consonants and vowels created the very same sentences I had read before. If you accepted Ted's basic chilling premise—which I was beginning to—then the rest played out with abominable logic. However, the basic question I had was, if Ted believed this, why send back the idol? Yes, Christians don't steal, but there were other items in play here. Theft seemed minor. About midnight I went to bed. I decided to take Ted's chapters to Pastor Haniford for a second opinion.

The next morning I checked with Deke and discovered the young couple had settled into a small house just outside of Americus, Georgia. Or, as Deke described it, what used to be an old storage shed renovated for residential use.

"They went right up to the main house and the folks seemed to know Ted. Shook his hand and hugged him like a long-lost relative," Deke said.

"He might have been," I said, recalling the pastor's words. I guessed Ted was a non-lost relative to the Georgia family.

"They drove onto the property. About two miles in, there was a little shack that seemed to have been fixed up. They're staying inside and out of sight."

"You have any company?" I asked him.

"Nope. Diego and I are keeping our eyes open. There's not much traffic in this part of Georgia. Nothing unusual. All the cars and trucks look rural and in place. You gotta love a truck with a rebel flag on it."

In this case I agreed with him. I was born in the South and have ancestors who fought for the Confederacy, but have no sympathy for the "Glorious Cause." Instead of getting half a million good men killed or wounded on battlefields, the South just should have shot all the slave owners. I admire the courage of the men in gray, and almost understand the officers and men who hated slavery but still felt they must take up arms to defend their homeland. Legally, they may have had a good case. If Rhode Island or Massachusetts were to secede today, would the nation kill residents of those states to keep them in the Union? Probably not. Morally, of course, my Confederate ancestors were wrong.

But today, I doubted anyone who wished Ted and Stephanie harm would have rebel bumper stickers on their trucks. I doubted too that they would be driving pickups. So, for a while, God bless those good old boys.

Deke's voice interrupted my train of thought. "Most of the area up here is flat land. My partner and I are perched on a shady knoll, which is the highest elevation around. No one can sneak up on our friends. You can see for miles here."

"Very good," I said.

I wanted some lighter reading, or lighter activity, so I dropped Ted's diary on my desk as I switched the television on to a baseball game. By the fifth inning I had almost forgotten Ted and the idol.

Then Geneva Canterley slammed open the door and burst

into the room. She held something wrapped in a white cloth. She stomped to the edge of my desk. Her eyes flashed with anger. The veins throbbing in her forehead looked darker blue than normal. A jackhammer couldn't have matched the decibels in her voice.

"It's destroyed! D— you! It's useless!"

"What is useless?"

She whipped away the cloth and plunked the idol down on my desk. It looked like it had been in a train wreck. Tiny black cavities appeared in the grin and mouth. The point of the sacrificial knife had eroded. Pinprick holes appeared in the arm and chest. The thigh on one leg had been sheared. I guessed some type of acid had eaten away at the black figure.

I couldn't help but grin. "Never put your trust in a god who's subject to corrosion."

She responded in a way that reminded me of my old Army sergeant during basic training. After the flood of abuse, she merely stared at the black figure, as if in disbelief.

I didn't mention that Ted Landers knew a great deal about chemistry. He probably knew which substance he wanted to use. Or maybe he'd created something just to use on the little Aztec.

"Hope they had insurance," I said.

"The money doesn't matter," she said, in as cold a tone as I've ever heard. She ripped open a pack of cigarettes and stuck one between her lips. "You're not too good in your job, Mr. Banyon. You were hired to bring back the idol intact."

"I did bring it back intact. It just didn't stay intact."

Another small, dark bit of the idol dropped off and fell to the table. I shook my head. "I don't think civilization will miss it."

She took one last look at the crumbling idol, then looked at me. If, as they say, looks could kill... "Landers might have done this. Or you. You will pay for this sacrilege."

I recalled her smugness when told Pastor Haniford had

given back stolen property. "Christians might be more cunning than you thought."

"Or you are."

"Or I am."

In slow, extended motion, she lit her cigarette while keeping her glare on me. She breathed in the smoke and the tangy scent floated through the office. "Four men. Four men were there."

I nodded.

"And they're dead."

"Well, three are in the cemetery." I edged toward the desk and put my arms on the desk calendar, while looking directly at her. "They thought they were better than they actually were. Sometimes the second-rate make that mistake."

She was silent for a moment. "We're not second-rate. We're professionals."

The dark smoke from her cigarette seemed to hang between us. Then she waved her hand and the cloud dissipated. "Where is the darling young couple? Would you happen to have them stashed somewhere?"

I shook my head. "I don't have them stashed anywhere. That's one thing I'm sure of."

She looked around. Her eyes focused on the two pictures I have on the wall. One is a Florida seascape and one is of a black Florida panther standing on a hollow log. He looked fiercesome but, somehow, also friendly. Or at least not dangerous. Not to me, not with my ability to communicate with animals. Even a snarling dog would stop and smile when I spoke to him. When I reached out my hand, he'd lick my fingers. When riding horses, there was always a sense of comfort between me and the mount.

Even in the wild, there was harmony between me and the wilder animals. The panthers, in particular, I loved. I saw them as magnificent, free creatures. True, they killed, but only for food, never for sport, or for ego, or for spite. Once, perhaps stretching my animal kinship to the extreme, I walked up to a panther, who perched on a log like the one in the picture. It took a while, and there were a few snarls of apprehension, but, finally, I stroked the panther's back. I told her she was beautiful. She gave an appreciative growl. I walked north, and she was headed south. But before she disappeared I waved at her. The forest echoed with her amiable reply.

But as I looked at Geneva Canterley, I knew there could never be rapprochement between us. She was more alien than the animals. Animals you could understand, from the joyous dolphins to the creeping panthers. But there was something incomprehensible about Geneva and Bolly.

She finished her visual inspection of the office. "I thought Tiffany might be here."

I was surprised. "Tiffany?"

"She's missing."

I sat back in my chair. She looked pleased that she had shocked me. But I didn't detect any real concern for Tiffany. She flicked the ashes off her cigarette again, then flashed a malicious smile. "I see you're surprised. I was thinking you might know where she was. Thought you might have her stashed somewhere too."

"I wish I did," I said. "How long has she been was missing?"

"This morning Carmen told me Tiffany's bed was made but some of her clothes were gone, as was a necklace Tiffany particularly liked. She must have taken it with her." She eased down in a chair. "I can see your chivalric attitudes take over. Carmen told me how you protected Tiffany from her father when you first went over there. You hated Gary from the start."

"Don't like him any better now. Wonder if Tiffany's boyfriend knows anything. Or maybe he went with her." A dark flash across her eyes told me I had surprised her. This time I smiled.

"Tiffany has a boyfriend? Impossible."

"Why is that impossible? She's intelligent and very good looking."

"Ah...it's..." Geneva shook her head. She almost dropped the cigarette butt. She cleared her throat, then sighed. "It's just that with Tiffany's depression, she has not shown much interest in boys. I'm sure at this stage of her life a boyfriend might be more of a hassle than help. A disagreement with a boyfriend could tip her off the edge."

"Actually, the young man seemed very nice. Plays football. Very nice manners. That's a rarity in teenagers nowadays."

"Yes, it is," she said, although the words sounded like they had been frozen and spit out like ice. "How do you know about him?"

I showed a sunny, beaming smile to counter her icy tone. "They came by the office. Tiffany wanted to ask about Stephanie."

Geneva said nothing, just chewed on her cigarette.

"But if you're concerned about the depression, Tiffany seemed free of it when she came in. She looked very happy. She smiled a lot and laughed a couple of times. The two of them made a nice couple. They were holding hands when they left."

Geneva gave me a blank look, so I clarified the remark. "Tiffany and her boyfriend. They were holding hands." I looked outside, toward the street. "I would like to make sure they're safe."

She snubbed out the butt, grinding it in the ashtray. "Yes. A white knight. Chivalry is dead, Banyon. It's about time you got that message."

"I'm holding a personal revival. I've always had a soft spot for the more romantic aspects of the fifteenth century. All that wonderful lyric poetry. Allen a Dale. 'Gather Ye Rosebuds While Ye May.' Ever read any Suckling? Nice little poet. Sadly, he died quite young."

Geneva scratched the corner of her mouth. "Of all the

107

drug-addicted, greed-heads, or ruthless ex-cons in the city, Bolly had to pick up you."

"I think it was my charming smile that persuaded him. Also, I don't think a drug-addicted greed-head could have helped him much."

She walked over and ran her hand gently along my jaw. The angry smile changed to a sweet one. "Ever heard the name Ashtaroth?"

"Can't say I have."

"She is mentioned in the Old Testament."

"Haven't read much of that. I know a little of the Psalms."

Her fingers kept gliding on my check, tracing the jaw line, as if she was giving me an extremely close shave. The cold voice melted into a soft, sensuous tone. "She is a goddess."

"Oh. Doesn't have many worshipers nowadays, I'm guessing."

"She has a small, but very devout following."

"I was raised Baptist myself."

Her fingers gently grasped my chin and she turned my heard toward her. "At certain times, during certain ceremonies, if you say ten special words, Ashtaroth will appear to you. The Greek myth of Medusa is based on her. She is awesome and terrible to behold. She has driven some men insane."

"If that's the case, I'm betting she doesn't have many boyfriends."

"Perhaps I shall send her to you. She likes to play. She can caress you."

"Thanks, but I prefer to hook up at a local bar. The ten magic words there are, 'Yes, I'd love to see the rest of your tattoo.' "

"You killed those other men with bullets, but there is no defense against Ashtaroth."

"Really? Should I ask Rev. Haniford about that?"

Her red lips spread into a wide, malicious smile. "His friend, the other pastor, is dead. His God couldn't protect him."

"Maybe the pastor just forgot to duck."

I had eased my hand underneath my jacket. I felt the cold handle of my gun. In a second I whipped it out and stuck the barrel under Geneva Canterley's chin. It knocked her back onto the desk. I rose from the chair and stuck one hand on the desk, while keeping the gun under her chin. Instead of her smile, I saw a slight blink of fear in her eyes.

"Since you threatened me, lady, why don't I just shoot you?"

The stench of fear came from her mouth. I jabbed her with the barrel until she choked. "What can your precious Ashtaroth do for you now? Want to see her face-to-face, Geneva?'

"You wouldn't...," she hissed. She shook her head, as if trying to hitch up her courage. "You wouldn't kill someone in cold-blood."

"Self-defense."

"No one will believe that."

"They don't have to. I'm the guy holding the gun."

I waited for about ten seconds, then yanked the gun away. She rolled off the desk. The barrel had left a circle of red on her throat. She stood up and walked back to the chair, where she picked up her purse. She stared at me. "Despite those macho tactics, I think we understand each other, Mr. Banyon. Don't give us any more trouble."

I grinned. "Bolly and you deserve one another. A match made in... well, not quite heaven, was it?"

She didn't smile, just turned and walked away. When she opened the door, she turned around. "By the way, you're fired."

The news wasn't surprising.

Then I remembered she had dumped the Aztec on my desk. I shouted at her, then pointed at it. "Don't forget your disabled god."

"See you in hell, Banyon."

When she slammed the door the office shook and another

black jot dropped onto the desk from the idol. I picked up the piece and the little Aztec god and dropped them both into the wastebasket. When the black figure hit, it crumbled into dust.

Seventeen

I pulled a bottle of bourbon out of the bottom drawer, and a glass, and poured a drink. Even Baptists would drink after a visit by Geneva Canterley. I dropped my gun on the desk. I let it lie there while I sipped the liquor. On the computer I called up the Volusia County website. I wanted to get a better look at the property belonging to Bolly Canterley. A plan was beginning to hatch in my mind.

I called Deke and got the jolly redneck accent a few seconds later. The happy couple had been relaxing and working, he told me. There was no sign of any trouble.

"You know what's wonderful about the country, Jarrod?"

"No traffic jams?"

"Precisely. Do you know in a rural area about three cars go by during an hour's time? It's very easy to keep watch when you can spot intruders from two miles away."

"I'm glad the couple made it easy for us. Now it may get harder."

I sensed the tension from Georgia. "What's up?"

I told him I wanted him to introduce himself to the Stephanie and Ted, but to mention my name when he did it. Assure them that their parents and that Danielsons did not know where they had fled. But I also needed them to get in touch with Tiffany and instruct her to get in touch with me.

"What's going on, Jarrod?"

"I will just give you the basics. Tiffany has disappeared, along with her suitcase and car. I'm going to check, but I'm

111

guessing her boyfriend, Frank Averill, is also missing. The last thing I want is for Tiffany to head up to Georgia to be with her best friend."

"Why not? We could keep watch over both of them."

"Yes, but Tiffany has a new car, given to her by her less-than-loving parents. I'm taking a wild guess and saying the car has devices that will allow her parents to track Tiffany."

Deke was silent for a moment. "That seems a bit paranoid."

"You don't know her parents, or the people they hang around with."

"With technology it's possible. Easy in fact. But..."

"Let's not take any chances. I think Gary or Carmen Danielson said something or did something to make Tiffany bolt. I'm betting the Danielsons think that, when Tiffany thinks she's safe, she will contact Stephanie, and the two will meet. Or Tiffany will head to wherever Stephanie is. These two have been best friends for more than a decade. So, if you're eighteen and have knowledge of the finest technology, couldn't you devise a way to keep in touch if you're separated?"

"Yes, I could. And in a way no one else could find out. But could they?"

"Both are intelligent and high-tech savvy."

He thought for a moment. "So what's your plan?"

"They can track cars, but no system can tell them who's driving that car. I want to switch cars with Tiffany and lead them on a wild goose chase."

Deke laughed.

"But I'm also going to need Diego. Can you handle it alone?"

"Sure. Besides, sounds like all the trouble will be down your way."

I eased back in the chair and poured another drink. Fortunately, I have a high liquor intake capacity. It takes a while before alcohol has an effect on me. Which is good, because I had a feeling I would need all my wits, all my strength, and all my cunning in this case. I swallowed half the liquor.

Even with all that wit, strength, and cunning, if Pastor Haniford's intercessors weren't first-rate, a lot of people would die, and I could well be one of them. That, I decided, was reason enough for a phone call.

The drive up to Duval County was uneventful, which was fine with me. I was beginning to enjoy uneventful afternoons. Duval County and Jacksonville is like almost everything else in Florida these days—too crowded. Still, the city fathers have made some improvements. The river section is beautiful. It's an entirely different city than the one that had the paper mills in the mid-twentieth century. Or the city run by the railroad barons. During that time, the newspaper stories never had trains hitting cars or pedestrians. The cars or people always slammed into the locomotives.

Pastor St. John Oberjan had a medium-sized church in the county, a bit smaller than Pastor Haniford's establishment. Knowing his background, I wondered if the church would have a Haitian decor, but the lobby and the sanctuary carried no special design. The pastor himself was six-two, dark as coal, with a big smile. He wore a white suit with a large golden cross around his neck. He had the most intense brown eyes I had ever seen. I wondered if his glare could slice through doors or see into the souls of his congregants. As I told my story, the brown eyes sharpened, flared at times, then calmed and became a smoldering fire.

I had copied some of Ted's diary and showed the pages to him. He had said very little during my tale. But his eyes revealed he was listening to every word. He had a gold letter opener shaped like a small knife. Occasionally he would pick it up and punctuate the move with an "ah" or "oh." Once he brought the tip of the opener beneath his ear and tapped it on his cheek.

He silently read the documents. He'd stop, flick the knife tip on the page, nod, and keep reading. When he was done he edged back in his chair, then leaned back. He moved the pages over to the side of his desk. I didn't say anything. He was thinking and didn't want to talk—at least that was my impression. He stayed motionless for a few minutes, then gave a slight nod and turned back my way.

"You must understand Mr. Banyon, that I came from a primitive culture, and a culture steeped in black magic and voodoo. It is the reason my native country is so poor and backward—forces of darkness have, in effect, ruled there for centuries. Do you know the stories of the Pilgrims and the Jamestown colonists?"

"A little."

He held the letter opener and he pointed the tip toward the ceiling. "For all their flaws, they set a cross on the ground and dedicated this new land to God. A hundred years later, an equally dedicated group of people dedicated Haiti to the devil. You can see the difference."

I nodded.

"I saw some horrible things while growing up around Port-au-Prince, but you must understand I know more about the African type of voodoo magic than about European black magic."

"There's a difference?"

"Oh, yes. The African tradition and type of magic are different than what you will find in the United States or Europe, but both are evil."

"I didn't realize...I thought black magic and Satanism

were...not real."

"They are very real, Mr. Banyon. There are not, thank goodness, a great many practitioners, but the number seems to be growing."

"Not a good sign for civilization."

He frowned. "No, it isn't."

I waited for a moment. He tossed the letter opener on the desk, then leaned back in his chair. He interlaced his fingers. "From what I understand, you have drawn certain conclusions from your experience in this case and from Ted Landers' suggestions and hints in his diary. Yet your conclusion is...incomprehensible to you."

"Yes," I told him. "Let's say I've never seen anything like it before in my life, and I thought I had seen a lot. If I told this to a psychiatrist..."

The pastor smiled. "He would dismiss Ted's views as those of an individual with many mental problems."

"Yes."

"But I've seen more than any psychiatrist on Earth and I, thank the Lord, still have the mind of Christ. In places like the one I grew up, you really appreciate the sacrifice of Jesus. You have first-hand knowledge of what our Savior saved us from."

I waited for him to continue.

"Your contention, Mr. Banyon, is plausible. It is possibly the most grisly example of the Black Arts, but I have known of such things in Haiti. In a nation such as the United States, where there is so much light, it may seem unbelievable. I only wish it was."

"Do you agree with my course of action?"

He was silent for a moment. This time the gold point tapped the corner of his mouth. "Yes. It might work...if we intercede for you, and we will be doing that immediately. You are, of course, in great danger."

"I know how to handle myself, Pastor."

"Not in this situation, you don't."

"Well, yes, there are some unusual aspects to this case."

"Unusual now, but perhaps not in the future. These are the end times, Mr. Banyon, the last days. In the end times the light will get brighter, but the dark will become darker. The manifestations of the Holy Spirit will grow and increase and, in my view, will flow in the land. But demonic manifestations will also grow and increase."

I remembered the Chinese proverb, "May you live in interesting times." It was both a blessing and a curse.

The ride back to Daytona Beach was also uneventful. Perhaps I had a streak going. For a man who thought he liked action, I was beginning to appreciate peace and quiet. In fact, after this case was over, I was hoping to have a totally serene life. I wanted the greatest future shock to be hitting the green on the first shot on the difficult par 3 ninth hole at Pinehurst, the country club I often played.

I drove into my garage as the sun settled onto the horizon, giving the evening an orange-pink glare. I opened the gate to the backyard, entered, and yelled for the dogs. Summer and Autumn barked with glee and ran toward me. I petted both when they leaped up to greet me. They are both a mix of Border Collie and Husky. Summer is a mixture of dark and white colors, with the dark more predominant. Autumn is just the opposite. She has a sparkling white coat, with small splatches of black. They gave a few more appreciative barks.

I filled up their food dishes and checked the water. Both dogs are beautiful animals but are somewhat spoiled. They both consider dry food to be only for emergencies…if they're really hungry. More often than not, they eat their fill of beef, chicken, or cube steak. If I need to leave the county on business, I have a friend who comes in to take care of them. There is a small shed on the property for cover in case of wind or cold, although it doesn't often get really cold in Florida. Being part Husky, they never seem to mind the cold. They are on dry food when I leave, which may be one reason they always seem overjoyed when I return.

I remember one episode of *Law and Order*, about a couple who had brutalized their dogs to train them to attack. The dogs learned too well and mauled a neighbor. The dogs had to be put down while the owners were sentenced to ten years.

"Seems a shame. Should be the other way around," was the last line on the show.

Yes, it should.

Of course, wild animals can be dangerous. It is not yet advisable for the lamb to lay down with the lion. If the pastors were right, perhaps someday...but not yet.

Eighteen

After dinner, I sipped a bourbon and Coke and went over the county maps again. I was familiar with a great deal of the rural space in Volusia, at least what little was left of it. I had roamed on much of it. I had even hunted around the outskirts of the Canterley property when I was much younger, not that I knew then who it belonged to. I'd assumed there would be a hunting cabin on the property where members would meet before going out.

The cell phone sang its melodic tune. I picked it up and this time heard a friendly voice. Diego seemed quite happy.

"I can save you a trip, my friend," he said, after telling me hello.

"Good."

"We did as asked. The young couple was a bit suspicious at first, but when Deke mentioned your name, they became friendlier. Trusting even."

"I'm betting your charismatic manner won them over too."

"Well, sure. That helped."

"Nice to have you on our side, Diego. On the other side, you could swindle old ladies and con young girls."

"Wouldn't do that. I'm a Christian. Did you know there are two priests in my family, on my mother's side?"

"Impressive. So why didn't you go into the priesthood?"

He laughed. "Not for me. But I respect my uncles. They're doing God's work."

"Which is never done."

"Anyway, it will please you to know I am heading to meet the other young couple."

"Tiffany and Frank."

"Yep. Where should I bring the car?"

I thought for a moment. "Meet me at Evergreen's, that restaurant between Daytona and Ocala, east side of the forest on State Road 40."

"I know it. Say tomorrow at three."

"See you then."

I turned back to the computer and Ted's underlined diary. Summer and Autumn are basically outside dogs, but tonight they rested comfortably on the thick, burgundy shag rug. I was in my study.

Down the hall is the living room and, beyond that, is what we in Florida call the Florida room, where I have the large TV and entertainment center. During the baseball season, there was little reason to leave the house. Technology is splendid. I am awed by the new medical devices, the new drugs, the high-tech equipment. I would enjoy seeing man go to the stars if scientifically feasible. And I wonder how we ever made it in life without a computer. But the finest technological innovation by far has been the Baseball Channel, brought by the local cable company. Usually about eight to twelve games a day are broadcast during the regular season. You can keep up with your favorite players while watching the rest of the teams too. My favorite team is the Atlanta Braves. Growing up, they were the closest professional team to Florida. During my teens, the Marlins arrived in Miami, but that was far away too. A few years later, the Tampa Bay Rays became the new boys on the block. I had to root for the Rays because they are a Florida team and also because they're always the underdog. Facing the New York Yankees and the Boston Red Sox, they are in a tough division.

Summer growled. Autumn's ears went back. Both glanced around. Summer got up and pawed the ground. Autumn followed and growled again.

"What is it?" I said.

I looked out the window but nothing was in sight. Everything looked peaceful. But the growling increased, deeper and angrier. Summer bared her teeth. I walked over and petted her head and neck.

"What is it, girl? Something out there?"

I have a first-rate burglary alarm, but it was silent. Yet the canine duo sensed something. I moved my hand toward my holster and grabbed my gun. I took a deep breath and looked around.

Summer barked again. Autumn paced frantically, then also yelped.

I felt something too. An odd sensation. A chill. Coldness swept the room. And something else. Something...evil.

Due to my military experience, I've known fear. Or I've known the emotion. Your training allows you to fight it down. This was different. There was nothing in the room, or outside that I could see, to fear, but the emotion crystallized, as if there was a fog in the room.

I moved out into the corridor.

Bits of light and grayness swirled at the end of the hall. Ripples of an ugly scent flowed over the house. The gray bits turned a dark, rancid green. More and more seemed to coalesce at the end of the hall. Finally, a dark figure morphed into view. A tall shadow.

I aimed my gun at it, aware that the term "skin creeping" was not an exaggeration. Summer and Autumn kept up their howling. The anger of their barks changed into a wail of despair. I shook. Along with the chill, a wind kicked up. But that was impossible. Yet the strong breeze took the green and gray bits of matter and stuck them to the dark figure. Slowly, a head and shoulders formed.

I fired twice, to no effect.

Then I realized the figure was moving, slowly, inexorably toward me. I looked around frantically. I was trapped. There wasn't a door in this part of the house. I wondered if I should bust a window.

I fired again.

I could barely make out the face of the astral intruder, but when she moved her lips, the hideous smile flashed through the darkness.

She had driven men mad, Geneva Canterley had said.

I kept firing until the hammer clicked empty. I knew I would die in seconds.

Then...then...

In a moment the apparition was gone, although I heard her agonized cry as she blinked out of sight.

My shaken knees couldn't support me. I slipped down to the floor. Immediately, Summer and Autumn stopped howling. They were soaked in sweat. So was I.

The chill evaporated, and the unearthly wind stopped too. A deep calm settled in the house. I raised my arms and Summer and Autumn came on each side. I rubbed their backs.

Later, I would tell Pastor Haniford what I thought had happened. It occurred so fast I couldn't be sure. But I thought, for a split second, there was a second apparition. The second was nothing like the first.

Tall and brilliantly white, the second apparition carried a sword. In less than a second, he swung it. When the blade touched the dark figure, she screamed in agony and disappeared. Then he vanished too. It had all happened in less time than the thump of a heartbeat.

An angel?

Sweat poured down my face. Drops fell on my shirt. I know deep inside that I owed Pastor Haniford and Pastor Oberjan another debt. It was not my quickness or my strength or my ability that kept me alive. Not tonight.

But I didn't think the night was over, not if I had read my adversaries correctly.

I herded the dogs into the study. I petted both for several minutes to calm them down. I later learned that some dogs are more sensitive to events in the astral realm than humans are. Gradually, they calmed down. Summer rolled over on her side. Autumn, tenser, sat on her stomach, legs outstretched. I told them to stay but left the door open, in case of emergency.

I went into the bathroom, found a small knife, and made a small incision on my forehead. Such cuts are not serious, but they do bleed profusely. I ripped my shirt and spread some of the blood on my back. Another small stream ran down my jaw. I wanted to give the visitors their money's worth. I had a hunch they would want to gloat—to see firsthand the remains of the man who, they thought, had cost them their precious idol.

I told Summer and Autumn to be quiet, then went into the living room and waited. When I saw the lights of the car, I smiled. I unlocked the door and switched off the alarm.

In the living room, I sprawled across the ottoman in front of a recliner. My left arm and shoulder covered it. I held my gun in my right hand that was covered by my body. Someone walking in should grab my left shoulder to turn me over. And when he did...

When the couple came to the door they were quarreling. It seemed to be a staple of the marriage, or whatever it was they had between them. I heard the door open.

"It's not locked," Danielson said.

"Careless of him," said his wife. "Although it wouldn't have helped."

I thought the Canterleys might come, but they had sent the

second string. Maybe the leaders stayed in safety, just in case. When they walked in, I could almost sense their huge smiles. Danielson even gave a low shout of triumph.

"Not so cocky now, are you, Banyon," he said, as I felt his hand on my shoulder, pushing me toward the floor.

As I turned over, I bent my leg. Landing on my back, I delivered a firm kick to Danielson's groin. His sharp cry died in his throat as I hammered his jaw with my gun. He fell like a sack of cement. After he hit the carpet, he didn't move.

In a second I was on my feet. The shock and surprise on Carmen Danielson's face was worth a million dollars. She opened her mouth, but no sound came out. Her eyes widened in fear. In what I thought was a quaint gesture, her hand went to her heart, as if wanting to assure herself she was still breathing.

"You're...you're...alive," she said.

"Yeah, I am."

With a viciousness I didn't realize was in me, I backhanded her savagely. She screamed and fell to the floor, rolling over. She lay still for a second, then forced herself up to her knees. I took several steps toward her.

"You know, I've never hit a woman in my life," I said. I eased down on one knee, the gun still in my hand. "I've never come close to hitting a woman. The nearest might possibly be when I pinched a girlfriend's rear end."

A stream of blood ran from her lips. The second slap knocked her to the floor again. She landed with a thud.

I looked at her with utter disgust. "I should say I've never hit a lady, but then, you are no lady, are you? Not by a long shot. In fact, I'm wondering if you're even a part of the human species."

I grabbed the back of her blouse and hoisted her up, then slammed her against a chair. The flow of blood from her mouth increased. The drops flowed down and spotted the green blouse. Her gaze blurred for a minute, then she gave a knife-piercing stare at me.

"Wanna talk?" I said.

She spat out a dollop of blood. It plunked on the carpet. "I'll tell you nothing, Banyon. Nothing."

I laughed. It wasn't the reaction she expected. A dark shadow of fear dimmed the angry stare.

"Don't be silly," I said. "If I decide to get rough with you, you'll tell me your mother's maiden name and anything else I want to know, including how many people you and Gary have murdered in the past."

"I never knew my mother, and I certainly don't know her maiden name. That goes for any other information you want too."

What I said was true. I had never hit a woman before and I felt guilty, even if the first woman I had hit was Carmen Danielson. That was one of the rules ingrained in me as a child. A man never hits a woman. On a scale of human scum, a man who hits a woman is only one step above a child molester.

Even if the people who made those rules never dreamed of any woman like Carmen Danielson, I still felt bad. I stepped back from her. There was still fear in her eyes, but the face was angry and defiant.

She shook her head and said, "Whatever you do, I won't tell you anything. Whatever you do, there are people...who will do much worse."

I walked back toward the other side of the room and sat down in a chair. I glanced toward Gary, but he was still out. I didn't think he'd regain consciousness until the morning.

I shrugged. "I'm not sure I know enough to ask the proper questions, besides asking who your co-conspirators are. But I think I know two of them, so the rest are a moot point." I walked toward her and knelt down on one knee. I looked her directly in the eyes. "But you won't get Stephanie back, and you won't get Tiffany back."

"We'll see about that."

I walked back to the chair and sat down again. "You're not as good as you thought you were, you and Gary. You underestimated the young couple, and you overestimated your own abilities."

Her hand came up to wipe away more blood. "And we underestimated you. No one else I know has ever survived a visit by Ashtaroth."

"I can't take credit for that one. You underestimated a couple of pastors too."

She said nothing, just sighed. Her purse was in the middle of the floor. She reached for it, but I pointed the gun at her. "Don't do it," I said.

"I just wanted my cigarettes."

I walked over, picked up the purse and opened it. I turned it upside down and let the contents fall to the floor. I picked up the cigarette package, turned it over, then flipped it to Carmen. She caught it in the air. When she stuck a filter in her mouth, I tossed her a lighter.

For a minute, we looked at each other through the smoke. I leaned back in the chair. I glanced at Gary again. He looked like a figure from an old Popeye cartoon. "As a matter of curiosity, just how did you keep Bluto away from Tiffany all these years?"

Her cigarette's end flared as she drew in the smoke. "Bluto knows his place. Once in a while he forgets. He tends to crumble under pressure. When he forgets, he is reprimanded, quite severely. Many years ago, he spent three days in what we call 'the chamber.' He has never forgotten the experience. Once, when Tiffany was about eight or nine, she walked into the living room after taking a shower. She was wrapped in a white bathrobe. Gary, tongue hanging out, started to remove it. I told Tiffany to go to her room. Then I reminded Gary of his time in the chamber and told him there could be a second time. He literally went white and begged me to forgive him. He was on his knees on the carpet crying, weeping for mercy."

"Must have been a real happy family."

"Gary has been very valuable to our group. He is actually very good at his job, which is one reason why, when he makes mistakes, the punishments are less than lethal."

"He finds all the ugly idols?"

She nodded. "That's one part of his job."

"There is one thing I'm curious about," I said. "You have a lot of ugly little figures at your shop. Why was this one particular artifact so important?"

Carmen lit her cigarette but said nothing.

I shrugged. I figured she wouldn't answer, but after taking a puff on the cigarette, she said, "You're intelligent. Take a guess."

I smiled. "But whatever it was, it doesn't matter now. The idol is no longer available for service."

Her voice was as cold as a cemetery tombstone. "That was the preferable object. The most perfect one. But we can use others."

I reached to a small end table and picked up a cell phone. "I wonder if I should call the police. This is a home invasion."

She shrugged. "The door was open. You assaulted us."

I reached down and picked up her keys. "Come on, lady."

She stood up. I called Summer and Autumn and they came running. I grabbed Gary by the collar and hauled him to the door. Then, with Summer and Autumn, I walked Carmen to her car. She stood by the side of it while Summer and Autumn guarded her. I went back and dragged Gary to the car, opened the back door, and pushed him in. Then I flipped the keys to Carmen.

"Good-bye," I said.

For a moment, she just stood and looked at me. There was no fear now, only amazement. She held the car keys as if they were an alien object. Her voice, so strong before, quivered. "You're letting us go?"

126

"Yes."

I knew what she was thinking. She was remembering my flush of anger, and what I had wanted to do to her. For a moment, a splash of sympathy washed over me. I guessed it wouldn't have been the first time she had been beaten and mistreated by men.

That still doesn't excuse evil. And it didn't excuse the fact that she and her friends had tried to kill me, with an extremely unpleasant death. I felt the anger rise again but, for just a second, kindness appeared in her gaze. There are streetlights on our avenue. The glare from one flashed over a tree, so her face reflected both light and shadows. Sometimes such a juxaposition can make someone look old. But in my mind's eye, as the light played on her figures, I saw her as young, as a child, before the world took her down. There was an innocent smile on her face, laughter on her small lips, and wondrous eyes that looked with curiosity on the world.

Oddly, there was no defiance now. Just an unsteadiness, almost a fragility instead of the diamond confidence she had always showed. Her hand moved slowly, and one finger wiped away another dab of blood from her mouth.

"If this had gone the other way, Banyon, we would have killed you."

"I know."

She looked at her hand and the fingertip of blood as if it was something new to her—like a child who is not seriously hurt, just curious about pain and blood. "On our side, mercy is considered weakness."

"I'm not on your side."

She looked unsure and leaned back on the car with a puzzled expression.

I was a bit puzzled myself. "Something happened in that house. Something saved me. I know it was put in motion by Pastor Haniford and his people. I just figured I wasn't saved in order to be cruel to others, even to enemies."

She shook her head, as if she couldn't comprehend my statement.

I wasn't sure I understood it myself. I holstered my gun. "One question, Mrs. Danielson."

She nodded.

"I have only a limited knowledge of...your side but when you attempt something like that..." and I gestured toward the house "and it fails, isn't there a reaction? A blowback? In other words, to put it bluntly, why are you still alive?"

She gave a sour smile. "There are...precautions we can take, in case of mistakes."

"If a mistake kills you, doesn't that tell you something about the creatures you're dealing with? Perhaps you should quit."

The sour smile widened. "It is too late, Mr. Banyon." She opened the door and got in the driver's seat. She inserted the key in the ignition.

I moved a step closer. "It's never too late, Mrs. Danielson. Not until we draw our last breath."

She turned toward me. "I drew my last breath a long time ago. On that initiation night when, as a child, I was offered to the coven...and they all took up the offer. That was my last breath. It's just a matter of time until they close the coffin."

"I'm sorry I hit you, Carmen. Forgive me."

She leaned back and gave a dry, mirthless laugh. Then a long sigh came from her. "You know no one has ever said they were sorry to me. No one ever asked forgiveness from me. And now it comes from a man I tried to kill."

"Life is strange, isn't it?"

She started the engine and backed out of the driveway.

I stood and watched as the car lights receded into the darkness. *It's never too late, Mrs. Danielson,* I thought, *because I know a pastor who deals in miracles.*

128

Nineteen

The next morning I patiently explained to Pastor Haniford the events of the previous night. It was a bright, golden Florida morning when I drove to his church. As I watched the cars go by, read the billboards, and observed the tree branches swaying in the wind, the previous night seemed like a dream. I shook my head. There was a much thinner line between reality and...even more reality than I had thought. Not, of course, that I had ever thought much about it.

Which is why I spoke slowly when I told the pastor of the hallway confrontation the night before. Speaking in the sunlight, in a church, with the pastor sitting in front of me, it seemed like I had stepped out of a different dimension—a very stark and terrifying dimension. For a second, I feared that Pastor Haniford would give me a condescending smile, pat me on the head, and secretly phone the mental health counselors.

But he didn't. He listened just as patiently as I explained. Once in a while, like a skilled military interrogator, he would ask a question. Once or twice he asked me to repeat something. I thought the most interesting part of the story was the apparition in the hall, but he seemed more interested in the conversation I had with Carmen Danielson. He wanted me to repeat almost every line I said to her and what she replied. I repeated some lines two and three times before he was satisfied. He asked how she looked and how she sounded. I was baffled, but then realized the pastor thought the lady might be a candidate for conversion. Which baffled me even more.

"You people try to save everybody, don't you?" I said.

He smiled, then showed a genuinely puzzled stare. "Yes, of course. That is our aim. It sounds like, in spite of everything she's done, or been through, that Carmen Danielson may be receptive to the gospel."

I shook my head. In his own way—albeit a much better way—Pastor Haniford was as incomprehensible as the hallway creature of the night.

"I was praying with our intercessors last night," he said. "And about the time you mentioned, we felt a ripple in the spirit. That's about the best way to describe it. A certain wave of demonic power. We prayed against it until it dissipated, but we had no idea of the specifics. Nice to know we were effective. I don't doubt St. John and his people felt the same thing and also wrestled in the spirit."

"I appreciate it."

"But I gather the struggle is not yet over."

"No," I said. "Not yet. Soon, maybe."

On the State Road 40 drive to Evergreen's I sadly drove through land that used to be covered in citrus trees. Not anymore. The state is losing about a hundred thousand acres a year of citrus land. The profits in development are simply too high to sustain agriculture. Some Florida families have been growing oranges and grapefruits and tangerines for generations, but when a developer offers fifty thousand an acre for their two-hundred-acre spread, they cannot turn down that type of money. Not when there are droughts and floods and pests and citrus cankers to face every year. Harvest is so uncertain. The developer's check is a sure thing. It's easy money. They have worked hard during the decades. Why not take it? So we are losing more and more trees and fruit but are getting shopping centers and housing projects in return. Where do you get orange juice when there are no more orange trees because they have all been bulldozed?

One of my childhood friends' grandfather served for two terms in the Florida House. Robert admired and respected his grandfather and often asked him about his legislative days. Once, the late Sumner Carter Emlet told his grandson that he had voted yes on a citrus bill. Why? his grandson inquired, knowing his grandfather knew next to nothing about the state's main crop.

"But I knew Doug Matthews from Orange County," Emlet said. "He was a good man and had a lot of citrus growers in his district. When he told me this bill was needed, and it was good for the state and good for the growers, I knew it was true. I told him I'd back it and we shook hands on it. That was that."

A simple handshake. That was an unbreakable promise back then. Both Sumner Emlet and Doug Matthews were men of integrity. Their word was gold. Twenty-four-carat variety. Once they gave you a promise and shook your hand, they'd die before they'd break their word.

And now...

Men like that have been ripped up like the abandoned citrus trees. Sold to the highest bidder.

I've always wondered if tough times produce tough, honest men or if the era you live in is immaterial. The greatest generation of World War II certainly saw tough times. They had to battle a depression long before they fought the Japanese and the Nazis. In the early 1900s in Florida, before the invention of pesticides, a man could stick his hand out of his window and see his arm grow black with mosquitoes. Those settlers fought the flying pests, the sun, the humidity, the scoundrels, the greedy merchants, the diseases, and everything else that came their way and produced a remarkable state.

Now, it seems, we are letting it slip away. Or had let it slip away. Past tense. I wondered if Montana was still pristine and beautiful. Or Idaho. Or parts of Wyoming. Or were people rushing to those states too?

Even so, I wouldn't leave. This was my piece of ground, my place under the sun. I had seen its beauty, been awed by the sunsets, thrilled by the dawns. I had walked its forest paths until I almost became one with it. I never liked the cities or the concrete or the asphalt, or the traffic. Or the sheer hustle of city life. I supposed some people can see beauty in skyscapers and feel awed in their presence. Ayn Rand certainly did. But I would not throw myself down to save a skyscraper. A dog, yes. But not an ugly building.

Once when I was about twelve, a friend and I were fishing in a canal. A car drove by and a man dropped a brown paper sack into the water. It kerplopped on the surface and went on down. I dove into the water, swimming with a fury I didn't know I possessed. Fortunately the canal wasn't too deep. I went under, spied the sack, and grabbed it. With my pocket knife, I ripped open the top, grabbed the black puppy, and we sped for the surface. I hoped he had not been in the sack too long.

A second after we hit the surface, he was licking my face.

We had enough dogs at my house, but we found him a good home.

Of course, we kill small humans now too, and dispose of them as rapidly as did the driver who dispatched the adorable, black puppy.

I trust humans are not silly enough to hope for a golden age. We're never going to get there.

I turned into the parking lot at Evergreen's and spied Tiffany's blue Toyota. Inside, Diego waited at a corner table. He munched a huge hamburger and had a plate of fries beside him. He waved me over. When I eased down, I ordered a smaller burger from the smiling waitress. She had a pale green uniform and spoke in Spanish to Diego before heading back to the counter.

"A companion?" I asked, as I slid into a chair.

He nodded. "She is helping to support her family. They came here about five years ago. Her older brother is now in the army. There are seven in the household, or used to be before her brother left."

"Wow. I was an only child."

Diego smiled. "You missed a lot."

"A lot of noise and arguments."

"And laughter. And tears. The youngest in her home is a brother, who is five, but is very smart. Good with numbers."

"Then he will have a bright future."

He nodded.

I glanced toward the parking lot. "You must have found Tiffany."

"Yes. The couple is going toward Americus to see Stephanie and Ted. Deke figured it would easy to keep an eye on both couples at once."

"Sounds like a plan."

"But it will increase your bill. Deke found a former army buddy up there who's helping him with the bodyguarding. Even Deke has to sleep sometimes."

When the waitress brought me an iced tea, I thanked her.

"So when will they be safe?" Diego asked.

I paused. "When we kill a few people or...when I find proof that will put those people away for life."

Diego stabbed a forkful of fries. "Try the second one. Deke and I don't do murder."

"Neither do I. Sort of limits our options, doesn't it?"

"Yeah. Kind of a shame. So, you know where some proof might be found?"

I wiped my mouth with a napkin, after swallowing a bite of my burger. "They have good food here."

"Good service too," Diego said. He watched as the waitress strolled to another table, then turned back to me. "The proof?"

"It's just a hunch, but I know a place where it might be found." Diego edged closer to the table and tilted his head my way. "The Canterleys own a great deal of property in western Volusia County, and their acres flow into Marion County, perhaps bordering the Ocala National Forrest. They also have a cabin on the property, although from what I've been able to discover, it's much larger than a cabin—unless you consider a two-story house a cabin. Canterley said he was a member of a hunt club. The house might be a place where all the members meet before the hunt."

Diego nodded. "Seems reasonable. Could also be a place to drink a few before going. Not a good idea..."

"Yeah, all we need is drunken hunters. But they might lift a few glasses when they return after the kill. I want to see the house, and I want to check the surrounding property."

"What do you think is out there? They wouldn't leave anything incriminating around."

"They might, as long as they feel it's a safe place."

Diego shrugged.

"If someone is out there, it could be tied rather easily to Canterley, I would think, since it's on his property. He goes out there all the time, He could claim innocence, but it would be enough to start an investigation."

I told Diego to take the car and take I-95 and drive it up to Georgia. Ninety-five because I wanted him along the east coast, and nowhere near Americus. He said he would circle back and meet me at the property after he ditched the car.

I grabbed the check when the waitress brought it and left her a big tip. Diego smiled.

"One thing, amigo."

"Yes."

"Does it matter if I drive the car, or someone else?"

I shrugged. "Doesn't matter, I guess."

"I have some friends over in Jacksonville. They will help me out. Could get one to drive the car up to Georgia and drop it near the South Carolina line. He could take the bus back. That way I could meet you sooner."

"Sounds fine to me. Perhaps we can get this wrapped."

He smiled. "They are a fine bunch, the couples we're watching. They hold hands while walking. You can see the love between them." He said a few words in Spanish in a sweet tone, then smiled again. He pointed at me, then jabbed himself in the chest. "Let's hope we can find such a woman, amigo."

"But let's get one with better parents."

"You know, they do not stay together at night."

I took one last drink from the tea. "No, I didn't."

"Very loving. But very dedicated Christians. She goes to the main house at night." He launched again into his sweet Spanish. I assumed it was another ode to young love and religious beliefs. "Seems strange."

"Well, fifty years ago it wouldn't have. Forty years ago it wouldn't have. But today, in society, it does. Society has changed. What does that say about them, or about society?"

He snapped his fingers and made a clicking sound as he grinned. "A sinful world, amigo."

"Yes, but, alas, it's the only one we've got."

"But one day, amigo, there will be a new heaven and a new Earth."

I stood up. "Until then, we have to deal with the old heaven and the old Earth and a lot of sinful inhabitants."

I drove slowly back to Daytona. It was getting late so I wasn't rushing. I wouldn't trespass on the Canterleys' property until tomorrow. I also wanted one question answered. When I got back to the city, I drove to the health club. I checked my watch. Usually J. Charles Sullivan was doing his workout about this time. He wasn't on the floor, but I spied him in the sauna. I changed to a bathing suit and walked in. He waved and gave me a huge smile. I sat on the wooden bench next to him.

J. Charles is one of the finest criminal attorneys in the state. Now he usually advocates for white collar felons. He can be tempted by an especially juicy murder case, such as the one a year ago when the grieving widow—who stood to inherit $57 million of her husband's money—was accused of shooting her spouse nine times and leaving a suicide note with the body.

The case was unique, but even J. Charles's eloquence could not convince the jury that the wife was innocent. The state had an ample amount of forensic evidence and testimony that her husband planned to divorce her. He had, in fact, picked out a diamond engagement ring for another woman. Since most people agreed that, without the $57 million, the husband was no prize, and wasn't much of a prize with it, the jury came back with a second-degree verdict. The judge was lenient and gave the defendant a minimum of fifteen years. It was something of a victory for J. Charles.

He had hired me a few times to seek information in several of his cases, including a particularly bitter multi-million-dollar divorce case. He represented the wife, who wasn't quite as bad as her husband. I agreed to the case, and it turned out to be one of the most profitable cases I ever handled.

But I wanted to clear up any possibly sticky legal questions with the legal master. One of J. Charles's strong points is he doesn't look like a sleazy lawyer. He's tall and thin and has an elegant bearing. The hair is mostly silver now and he has a silver and black mustache that gives him a dignified air. He smiled as he listened.

"So, you see, if I find evidence of a criminal conspiracy, I want to make sure it can be used in a trial, and that no sleazy legal scum, er, excuse me, no devoted defender of civil liberties, can get it tossed," I said.

He laughed. "I always suspected you had a strong belief in the Fourth Amendment."

"Actually, my favorite is the second, but I won't split hairs, or amendments."

He wiped sweat from his brow with a bright red towel. "Jarrod, if during the course of your investigation you happen across some evidence of a crime, you are obligated to go to the authorities. If a client enters my office and tells me, yes, he killed his mother-in-law and hands me the gun he shot her with, I take the gun to the state attorney. Even though I am a legal adversary of Tod Hamilton I remain an officer of the court. If you uncover evidence of a crime, and turn it in, no lawyer could get it tossed."

"Even if I were on the property illegally?"

"Even if you were on the property illegally."

"But there was that famous case up in Rhode Island some years ago. A private detective uncovered evidence, but it was ruled inadmissible, and a guilty man walked free."

He cleared his throat and moved into his pedantic mode. Occasionally J. Charles lectures at nearby law schools and colleges. "In that particular case, a judge, rightly or wrongly, determined the detective was a de facto employee of the state, and of the district attorney's office, and therefore he should have obtained a search warrant before entering."

I shook my head. "I don't mind sleazy lawyers. I mean, you expect lawyers to be sleazy, no offense..."

"None taken."

"But why do idiot judges buy arguments like that?"

"Jarrod, you do not understand the finer points of our legal system."

"No, I don't. I just want to lock the guilty up and protect the innocent."

"Easier said than done."

"Tougher than it should be due to some members of your esteemed profession."

"But I take it you are not acting in conjunction with the state attorney here."

"Nope. He has no idea what I'm doing."

"But the owner of the property is no longer your boss."

"He was biased about my services."

He leaned back and wiped his face with a towel. "But you believe several young people to be in danger?"

"That is a concern of mine."

"Then, in my opinion, you are on firm legal ground. Any evidence you may find that is connected with a crime can be given to the state attorney without any worries. He and his staff are first-rate attorneys. I'm sure they could argue persuasively that the evidence should be used. Not even I could get it thrown out of court."

I smiled. "Thank you. Of all the sleazy lawyers, Jay, you are the sleaziest, so to speak."

He nodded.

Twenty

The next morning, gray angry clouds rolled over Daytona Beach and Volusia County. Empty soda cans whistled across the asphalt and skidded down the streets, blown by the furious winds. Random sheets of newspapers also flew by. The winds caused the temperature to drop. As I looked toward the Atlantic I knew the bikini-clad tourists of yesterday were bundling up today. Or maybe just wearing long pants and a light jacket.

The cell phone buzzed and when I flicked it open, I heard Diego's voice.

"The car is headed to Savannah and I am headed toward you," he said.

"Boy, you're good," I told him.

I closed the phone and slid it back into my pocket.

Thunder crackled in the distance. The air smelled of rain. I eased a gray London Fog jacket over my green shirt and brown holster. The beretta was packed tightly into the ankle holster. I pulled back the curtains and peered outside. The storm was from the north, but it was headed this way.

I've always relished storms. I've enjoyed the thunder and lightning and rain. I've always felt a great sense of security in the midst of geophysical chaos. Of course, there are limits. Like any sane person, I'd head up I-95 if a category five hurricane came toward shore, or even a category four. But the typical Florida storms always made me smile. Don't know why. Perhaps one of my parents told me such squalls were a display of God's ability. If so, I wanted Him to show off more often. Many times I have experienced great joy just watching nature's awesome display of lightning and thunder.

"And God grieved that he had made man on the earth. For the wickedness was great and every intent and thought of his heart was evil." You can understand how He felt. So He sent a great storm to cleanse the earth. One of the passages I remembered from my Baptist upbringing.

That and one other passage from Genesis. Something that, to me, was incredibly puzzling, but I have never heard a sermon on it. The question of Satan in the garden. Most of the sermons are focused on the temptation. Forget the controversies over whether the first three chapters record an actual event or are allegories to gleam spiritual lessons from.

Why did God allow Satan to roam the earth? In Baptist theology, which I assume is Christian theology, there was a rebellion in heaven. Satan lost. He and a third of the angels were defeated and tossed below. But why did God allow him to linger on the earth? I do recall the Scripture that states hell was made for Satan and his angels. So why didn't God just drop his enemy in hell after the rebellion failed? The place was made for him. The result of not doing so has been six thousand years of pain, suffering, misery, and death. How many storms and floods are needed to cleanse the earth of six thousand years of innocent blood shed by evil men? Is there enough water in the world?

A few sprinkles hit the car's windows as I drove onto the street. Before heading west I wanted to drop by Souls Harbor. When I entered the parking lot, I saw another car, the one owned by Carmen Danielson. It was as incongruous as the Titanic in the Sahara. When I walked in, I saw the same friendly secretary I had when I had entered a week ago. She gave me the same friendly smile.

"Pastor Haniford and the woman you described are in one of our prayer rooms," she told me. "Two deacons and several of our prayer warriors are with them. The woman was crying, but it was a cry of relief, almost of joy, if you understand. We get a lot of that here. The group still has some ministering to do to her." Then the recognition hit.

"Are you Mr. Banyon?"

I nodded.

She reached behind her and gave me an envelope. "She asked me to give you that."

I ripped open the envelope and took out the single sheet of yellow paper. Carmen Danielson had fine, exquisite handwriting. In ornate letters, she had written:

Once you asked me to forgive you, Mr. Banyon. Now I ask you to forgive me. Forgive me for what I tried to do to you. Perhaps, as you said, it is not too late.

   Please save Tiffany.

For a while I just stared at the paper. I looked again and again at the little blue letters on the yellow paper. Carmen Danielson did not dot her I's. She made little circles above them. There were several faded, light stains on the sheet. I wondered if she had been crying when she wrote the note. I could not believe the woman who had been so hard and cold, and so murderous, could be redeemed.

But Pastor Haniford believed it. I shook my head. Perhaps no man, or woman, is beyond redemption. Perhaps her heart wasn't totally callous. Maybe there was a glimmer of that little girl left, before the coven took her.

Perhaps Carmen Danielson always realized her god was a devil, but still thought there was no way out. Until Pastor Haniford came on the scene. I smiled. Perhaps he, not my old commander, was the toughest armadillo on the planet.

After leaving State Road 60, I drove slowly down a number of dirt roads. Occasionally a spurt of sprinkles would slap the windshield. I figured the edge of the Canterley property was at a huge oak tree where someone had nailed a wooden sign. Faded red letters informed stragglers that this was *PRIVATE PROPERTY, KEEP OUT.* It wasn't the main entrance. A six-foot, barbed wire fence stood behind the tree. I halted the car and climbed out. I spied a random branch on the ground and picked it up, then tossed it on the fence. No buzz and no sparks. I reached onto the backseat of the car and brought out the wire clippers. The wire was old. It didn't take much strength to clip the wires. The blades came down with a solid clap as it cut the wires. I drove through.

It was a winding road but drivable. Ten minutes later the house came into view. A two-story, functional abode, with two sun decks. I stopped the car beneath a tree. The front door was locked, but it wasn't much of an effort to break in. If a private detective can't open a locked door, he should give up the profession.

It had a large ground floor. Two brown sofas were angled around an empty fireplace. A fireplace? In Florida? A magnificent deer head with large antlers glared down from above the fireplace. It was a shame. I would have liked the deer better than the hunters. Perhaps deep in the galaxy, on the planet Nmiron, deer are gathered in a room drinking and talking and there are human heads on the wall behind them.

A portable bar stood against a wall. I noticed it was well-stocked. I picked up a bottle of Scotch and noticed it was half-full. That alerted me to the fact that the living room and kitchen did not have much dust or the stench of a long abandoned house. The hunters had gathered here quite recently.

I glanced at the stairs but passed on checking the second floor. I turned into the kitchen. At the end of the corridor was another door. I slid it open. The steps headed downward. Who has a basement in Florida? My fingers fumbled around on the wall until I found the light switch. A single bulb flicked on. As I eased down the stairs, I reached into my holster and brought out the gun. The stairs led to another narrow corridor. Two wooden doors were on each side as I walked down. I tested the doorknob of one. It wouldn't move. I stepped back, then kicked it in. It flew open with a loud crash, then banged against the wall. I pulled out a flashlight and flashed it around the room.

A thousand needles began to prick my skin. The hair on my neck stood at attention and shouted messages to my brain to flee. A heaviness settled in the air. When I walked in, the air had been thick with rain. Heavier, darker material now filled the atmosphere. When the flashlight highlighted the chains and the random instruments of torture, I guessed I had found what Carmen Danielson had called the chamber.

I exited and moved down the hall. I took a deep breath and shook myself. From some place, a stench wafted toward me. A horrid smell. It made my eyes water. The oppression came in waves now. It seemed like I was walking through water, trudging along, fighting resistance every inch of the way. The airy ripples brought a wave of fear, then drew back and rushed back in a wave of anxiety. I kept looking behind me. Something was watching me. I was sure of it. The pulsating waves grew stronger.

The absolute stench of evil.

No other word for it.

There was an even deeper level. Down two steps I found myself on a platform. There was a light switch here, the one modern accommodation for an ancient practice.

About eight feet in front of me, bathed in dim light, stood an altar. On the wall in back of it was the most hideous painting I'd ever seen. The artist, if one can call him that, painted in black and bright red hues. The figure must have been eight feet tall. It had the head of a goat but a huge, misshappen human body, Naked to the waist, two large breasts gave the creature a perverse look. Its hands were clawed and hairy. Instead of human legs, it had the brown, hairy legs and hooves of a goat.

Talk about ugly personified.

I moved over to the altar. Dark stains covered a great deal of the surface and ran down the sides. I knew what the dark stains were. The hairy goat-god had wanted sacrifices.

I edged back toward the door. I had what I wanted. I would swear to the state attorney that I had found bloodstains in the Canterleys' hunting lodge. That should be enough for a search warrant. Forensics, I had no doubt, would establish the stains as human blood, and the Canterleys would be facing a series of tough questions. Police teams would also search the property, which I figured would turn up a body or two. Or possibly more.

The goosebumps were piling on goosebumps as I climbed the stairs. I was in so much of a hurry when I rushed back into the kitchen that I didn't notice the three men with rifles standing there.

Bolly Canterley stood there too, smiling. He wore a tan hunting jacket with a brown vest. His rifle leaned on a wall beside him.

"Mr. Banyon, so you've found our secret."

I said nothing.

"Take his gun," Canterley said.

A tall, ugly man with a scar on his cheek walked over and

relieved me of the Glock. I gestured to the assembled group. "The hunt club?"

"Yes. And you will see us in action."

When they motioned I walked out of the kitchen and into the living room. Eight or nine men looked toward me. They all had on hunting fatigues. Several carried weapons. I didn't recognize any of them. I saw three who looked like they were in shape. I guessed the other six hadn't spent much time in the gym. One man with an ugly tan had a hooked nose. Well-built, but he wasn't in any shape to do marathons. A pale, fat man with splotches of red in his cheeks stood next to Hook Nose. Not only was their god ugly, the followers weren't going to win any beauty contests either. A tall, Hispanic man stood in back of his two pale friends.

Canterley shook his head. "Hiring you seemed like such a good idea at the time."

"Perhaps Stephanie thinks it still was."

"Where is she?" Canterley said.

"Where you will never find her."

"Yes we will. We have abilities you have no conception of. It's only a matter of time."

I smiled. "Even if you do, it won't help. Your scheme, diabolic though it was, is over. All that careful planning has collapsed."

My words sparked interest. He frowned. His tongue flicked over the edge of his front teeth, like a predator licking his lips before pouncing on the prey. "What do you mean?"

"I mean Stephanie is not a virgin anymore."

Actually, I had no idea of Stephanie's sexual status, but I wanted to jar the group. Several gasps came from behind me. A rifle clicked. A few other men looked puzzled.

"It was a brilliant plan. Very chancy because of the time involved. A lot of things can go wrong in twenty-one years. And they did."

145

Canterley pulled back his lips. He had two rather pointed incisors at the edge of his mouth. "You don't know what you're talking about."

"Oh, yes I do. Ted Landers wrote it all down. Or most of it. He guessed the rest. He's a very bright young man."

"I knew we should have killed him." The voice came from the back of the room. Geneva Canterley stepped out of the shadows, a cigarette stuck in her mouth. She had the same cold-eyed stare she always had. I noticed another female in the group. A slender, black-haired woman with ebony eyes. Black-hair looked edgy, nervous. Geneva looked like she was at home. "There was always something about that boy," she said.

"Banyon is bluffing," Canterley said.

I stepped over toward the bar, and pointed to a bottle of bourbon. "You mind?" I said, looking at the charming couple.

"Go ahead, Banyon. It will be your last."

I moved around the bar, grabbed a glass, and set it down on the surface. I shrugged. "If it's my last, I'll make it a double." I didn't particularly want a drink, but a bottle can be a nasty weapon. I picked up the bourbon and poured the glass half-full. Two steps and I could smash the bottle in the face of Hook Nose. I still had the Beretta, but there were only six bullets in it. A desperate move, but it might have to be tried.

I took a sip, then smiled. "First, we have to assume that Pastor Haniford's theological worldview—and yours—is true. There is a God, a Redeemer, and a devil. Some people are devoted to one side and others are servants to the powers of darkness. Christians believe Jesus sacrificed once for all. In memory of that event, they take wine and bread. On the other side, the sacrifices are never done. They must be continually repeated. Satanists..." I pointed to a few of them. "That's what you all are, right?"

"That is one of the names we go by," Canterley said.

"Satanists don't mind sacrificing animals from time to time,

146

but the best sacrifice is a human. But some humans are better than others. There is a grain of truth in all those myths and legends about virgins being sacrificed to the dark gods. To release the maximum amount of power, to ensure that whatever goal you are seeking is obtained, a virgin is preferred." I looked at Canterley as I sipped the drink. "Am I getting warm here?"

He looked stoic. "Go ahead, Mr. Banyon."

"But there is this one coven who needed a human sacrifice for a unique ceremony. They planned it for decades. Satanists love astrology. Even before computers, a good astrologer could plot horoscopes and charts years in the future. I'm guessing in about three years, all those occultists are predicting there will be a very unique astrological configuration in the heavens. Perhaps such a planetary alignment might happen only once in a hundred years. Or perhaps only once in a milliennium."

I grabbed a stool and perched on it, then took a sip of the drink. "So if there is a coven that follows the black arts, how does it prepare for such an event? Something very, very special. That's where the virgin comes in. But the ceremony is even more specialized than that. The number seven has special significance to Christians. It's the number of perfection, the number of God. Three is also special, of course, because of the Trinity. But there is a satanic counterfeit for everything, so Satanists also place a high priority on the numbers seven and three. So three times seven is twenty-one. Three sevens. A virgin on her twenty-first birthday would be the ultimate sacrifice. In fact, for this particular ceremony, nothing else would do."I smiled and looked at Canterley. "Am I still bluffing?"

"Don't stop now," he said. "Please continue."

I drained the glass, then rapped it on the bar. "The problem is, where do you get one? Where do you get one in a culture your side has done its best to debase?" I grabbed the bottle again and poured another drink. "Here's the stroke of pure demonic genius. In a corrupt and decadent culture, you have to grow your own. *So you conceive a child just so you can kill her twenty-one years later.*"

A murmur went through the group. Several men, though, still looked baffled.

"By the way," I said, "just as a matter of curiosity, was that your idea, or did it originate with the goat guy downstairs who needs the D-cup?"

"He knows!" Geneva Canterley yelled.

Bolly Canterley took the news more calmly, although I did see another glimpse of the incisors as he drew a deep breath. "There are even members of our coven who did not know all the details of our plan."

"Shucks. Did I spoil the surprise?" I pointed toward the basement. "It was right down there, wasn't it? On that black altar."

I looked at Geneva. "It couldn't have been that comfortable. One night when all the group was here, did the others dance around the altar while you two...planned for the future?" I shook my head. "The ironic thing is that the child conceived by two of the most black-hearted people on Earth, under a picture of Satan himself and under a demonic spell turned out to be...one of the sweetest people alive. What would account for that? The grace of God?"

Geneva looked like she would spit on the carpet. "I never trusted you, even that first day."

I took another sip of the drink. "But the problem is, how do you keep a teenager a virgin when...er, moral teachings are not emphasized in the household? You just concoct a spell for the child. It creates an aversion to sex. Such a spell would be relatively easy for you all, I imagine. Then all you have to do is wait." I swirled the drink around in the glass. "But twenty-one years is a long time. You made sure Stephanie was introduced to Chad Atkinson, just so he could keep an eye on her. Were you suspicious? But the plan backfired. Chad wavered. Did he still

148

have some humanity in him? Then, some time later, Stephanie became interested in Ted Landers.

"Even so, her friendship with Ted didn't send off any warning bells, not even when she became a Christian. In fact, you may have been secretly pleased. For you, it was a delightful turn of events. You could not only sacrifice a virgin, you could sacrifice a Christian to your dark god." I shook my head. "Did you two have a good laugh about that? But the last laugh was Ted's. Ted's and his Lord's."

Canterley said nothing, but his dark eyes roiled with anger.

"Ted knew Rev. Tibbets, and Rev. Tibbets knew something about demonology. In fact his knowledge of the black arts was so extensive he began to get suspicious. That's why you had to kill him."

"He was a fool," Canterley said.

"His death came too late. He had already told Ted a lot of his insights. Ted figured out the rest for himself. So he took the girl he loved and fled."

The words came slowly from Canterley, as if he was straining at every syllable. "Stephanie is repulsed by sex. She would not..."

"That changed when she became a Christian. Happened to Tiffany too. Was Tiffany a backup, just in case something went wrong? Or were they both to be sacrificed?" I drained the rest of the glass. "What would the ceremony achieve?"

Canterley sighed. "It would have brought blood and death on such an enormous scale as to shake the nations. And great power for each member here."

I shrugged. "Such is life. The best-laid plans of mice, men, and Satanists. Maybe your side can think of something else by the time of the next unique astrological configuration. Say two, three hundred years." I snapped my fingers. "Oh, I forgot. Patience is a Christian virtue, isn't it? You probably don't have much of it on your side."

"Twenty-one years," Geneva said, her voice trailing off. "Twenty-one years..."

I looked around, but Hook Nose had moved away. Even if I tossed the glass and use the bottle as a weapon, at least five of the coven members held guns. The odds were not with me.

I raised my glass. "Although this turn of events can't make the little goat god happy. He was planning big-time for this and you failed." I looked around the room. "All of you. I've got a hunch your boss doesn't like failures. I imagine the punishment is...quite severe."

"You are lying. Stephanie is still a virgin. We will find her and bring her back, and we will find Tiffany too."

"Won't happen."

"There is no way you could know about Stephanie."

"Before I killed your three men—I'm guessing Gary hired them on his own—I talked to the couple. I know the glow of a young woman who just made love. It was on Stephanie that night. Rather touching and romantic." I dropped my voice a half-octave. "Now she's useless to you."

A low growl emanated from Canterley, but he said nothing.

I pointed at him. "But that's an interesting theological question. Christians don't believe in sex outside marriage. It's sin. But what if the joining was not due to lust, or any other sin? What if the sex was to save a woman's life? It's said God judges the heart. Ted's heart was right with the Lord. I'm sure Stephanie's heart was right too. So is that still a sin? Perhaps we should call a theologian. I'd be interested in the answer. How about you?"

Geneva Canterley let loose a stream of invective that would have embarrassed a sailor. Her husband looked at me. "They may have gotten away, but at least we can kill you, Banyon."

"Can't be much of a consolation prize."

"We—" Geneva said.

"No, we will kill him first," Canterley said. "Then we will

find Stephanie to see if he told the truth." He looked at me. "Look around, Banyon. We're predators and hunters. This house and property has been here for more than twenty years. Do you know how many people we have hunted down during that time?"

I said nothing.

"Almost two dozen. Sadly, the last three didn't give us much of a chase. They were too frightened. We tracked them easily and dispatched them. Perhaps you will be more of a challenge. When you are bleeding and we have gutted you, we'll ask again about Stephanie. If you convince us that you're telling the truth about her location, we will end your suffering. One of our victims lived three days with a bullet in the gut. He had remarkable staying power." He waved to several of his companions. "Bring him out."

Three men grabbed me and hauled me toward the center of the room.

"Get his ankle gun," Canterley said. A tall, slender man with curly gray hair lifted my pants leg and took the Beretta. He shoved it in his jacket pocket.

"You didn't think we knew about that, did you, Banyon? You'd thought you'd go out with an edge. We are not stupid."

"I never thought you were stupid. Evil, yes. Stupid, no."

"Take him out."

When we got to the door, they shoved me outside. I stumbled and fell into the dust. Rain had cut loose from the angry heavens. A steady drizzle hammered the earth. I picked myself up and turned around. The coven of hunters stood in a semi-circle around me. In the center were the Canterleys. Both held hunting rifles. Four men stood to Canterley's left. The one closest to him looked the most dangerous. Six-two, with a grizzled look. Lines cut deeply into his face but his manner and glare betrayed no age. Black curly hair fell down below his neck and forward to the edge of his heavy eyebrows. To his left was an older man. Middle-aged with a potbelly. His lips widened into a hideous grin that showed a jagged line of teeth. He was going to enjoy the hunt. To Mrs. Canterley's right stood the tall, thin man who had taken my Glock. It was still in his pocket. The broad-shouldered, pock-marked man next to him was shorter. His chubby hand held a Bowie knife.

I scanned the grim-looking group. "Only ten. I thought covens had more than that. Isn't thirteen the appropriate number? Oh, that's right. Carmen is no longer with you."

"We will deal with her later," Canterley said.

"Chad Atkinson left too."

"He paid the price for betrayal."

"Gary is not here either. Did he cut and run?"

"Gary outlived his usefulness."

"Two defections out of thirteen. That's not a good average. Perhaps it's due to lack of good leadership."

Canterley turned toward the chubby man with the knife. "When Altair guts you and empties your organs on the ground, we'll see how funny you are, Banyon. Now, take off your jacket and throw it to me."

I did as requested. Canterley gestured at one of the men. The man with the grizzled, chiseled face walked off, boots sloshing on the wet ground. A moment later I heard growls and barks. When he came back, he held brown leashes to two huge Doberman Pinchers. Both were black with two streaks of light gray across their back. They pulled and strained at the leash. When one saw me, he unleashed a ferocious howl and reared up on his back legs. As the man strained to hold the dogs, Canterley walked over and pushed the jacket toward them. Both sniffed it, running their noses back and forth along the sleeves and back. Blurs of black and gray sunk their teeth into the cloth and ripped the jacket apart. Their teeth looked as sharp as a chainsaw.

Canterley looked at me. His smile was almost as wide as the dogs. "Judas and Jezebel. They're trained to maim, not kill."

I could imagine the brutalization needed to create attack dogs.

"Usually, we don't use the dogs. We don't need them. But in your case, Mr. Banyon, we'll make an exception."

That explained something. Even with ten to one odds, even with the group holding all the guns, I questioned if they would turn me loose in the forest. The black Dobermans gave them confidence. Now I wondered if I should have smashed the bottle against the nearest Satanist's head and taken my chances inside.

He lifted his arm and looked at the gold watch on his arm, then glanced back toward me. "Sometimes we have given our prey a ten-minute headstart. With you...five minutes. Your time starts now."

Twenty-one

T he hunting lodge had been built on a slight hill. People who come from mountainous states would say bump. I ran down the slight elevation. The ground was open to my left, but a clump of trees was off to my right. The ground dipped slightly before rising again to meet the forest. Running with my best gait, my shoes hitting the ground solid, I guessed ninety seconds had passed before I dashed under trees. I turned left and got smacked by a low-hanging branch. I brushed it aside and headed into the forest.

I didn't doubt they had hunted down and killed other men. I guessed those men were not at home in the forest. Perhaps they were urban dwellers. Ten to one. If not for the dogs, I'd consider those pretty good odds.

First, though, I had to run, to put as much distance as possible between me and the coven. To put as much distance as I could between the two dogs and their masters.

I ran back into the forest, not bothering to zig-zig or do anything to hide my tracks. I had one very slim chance, but I needed time to pull it off. I hoped, not for the first time, that Pastor Haniford's intercessors were on the attack, spiritually.

In three minutes, after I sprinted around an oak tree, and dodged a pine, I saw what I wanted. I undid my belt. The oak tree looked weathered and old but sturdy. One branch looked about seven feet off the ground. I leaped up, felt the rough, stubby bark with my hands, swung my legs over and perched on it. I wound my belt around it, running the leather through the buckle. The rest of the belt hung down. Then I dropped to the ground. The splat when I hit sounded like a thunderclap. If what I planned failed, then there was a chance I could leap up, grab the belt and lift myself onto the tree, away from the dogs. Not a good chance...but when ten people armed with hunting rifles and attack dogs are tracking you, even a 10 percent chance of success looks pretty good.

My time had run out. I heard the Dobermans howling. It had to be my imagination, but I thought I could hear their paws running, spitting up mud and grass behind them as they raced. I'm still in good shape. There had to be more than a mile between my location and the hunting party. It would take the fat and out-of-sharp members a lot more than five minutes to cover it. Dobermans, of course, were a different story.

The howls came closer. Judas and Jezzy knew they had the right scent. My throat went dry as I heard the dogs frantically pawing the brush.

I moved under the hanging belt. It wasn't much of an escape route.

The snarling black shapes came into view. They raced out of the brush, then slowed, heads down, teeth bared. Now was the time to see just how good my kinship with animals was.

I tried to make my voice firm but friendly. "Judas," I said, "Jezzy."

At the sound of her abbreviated name, the female halted, and looked at me. Judas kept going, but he walked slower.

"It's OK. It's OK. I'm a friend. Friend. I know you never had one, but there's one here now." I had my hands out, palms open, and kept talking to them. "I know what they must have done to you, but I'm a friend. I won't hurt you."

Of course, they did not understand me, but I hoped they would respond to my voice. Jezzy shook her head. She growled, but she didn't advance. Judas barked and showed his fangs again. He circled, though, and did not move my way.

I took one step toward them, remembering the Florida panther. "It's OK. I'm not your enemy. I'm not the one who hurt you."

Jezzy gave a low moan, as I kept talking. Her eyes gave me the Carmen Danielson look.

"They abused Carmen when she was a child. Did they start brutalizing you when you were a puppy, Jezzy?"

Judas shook himself, then barked viciously. I kept talking, telling them it was all right. Pastor Danielson had mentioned a spiritual anointing and I hoped it was with me as I edged forward. I did notice a calmness and serenity in me and around me. Judas opened his vicious jaws, but the bark died in his throat. He looked puzzled, then shook his head. He circled his patch of ground again.

Jezzy gave a series of short yelps. Not angry. Not bloodcurdling. Not quite affectionate, but better.

"You're a good dog," I said, stepping close to her. "Other men have hurt you, but I won't. Good dog. We have the same enemies."

As I reached for her, the angry bark returned. I held my hand steady and spoke soothing words again. In the distance I could hear men rushing through the bushes. I took a deep breath and moved my hand toward Jezzy and stroked her. As I petted her, the tension eased out of her. I curled my arm around her and gave her half a hug.

"It's all right."

Judas walked over. He placed his head under my right hand and bumped it. I petted him and stroked his back.

The noise back in the forest increased. At least one man was close to us. I kept petting the dogs. "Would you like to change sides, guys?"

They didn't have a chance to respond. The grizzled-cheek man burst into the clearing. For a moment, he looked shocked, then he gritted his teeth in anger.

156

"Stupid dogs. I'll kill you too," he said as he raised his rifle.

Judas and Jezz charged.

They covered the distance between me and the hunter in two leaps, then pounced. He yelled in pain as Judas sank teeth into his neck. As he fell to the ground, the two dark shapes covered him, growling for blood. He tried to fight off the dogs, but they were too strong for him. Their jaws closed on his face and throat. A splatter of blood dotted my shirt.

I grabbed his rifle, felt the cold barrel and the wood stock. A feeling of great comfort.

The hunt had changed.

Now this was my ground, my territory. Long ago, I took my stand on Florida turf. I knew I would be on this magnificent piece of Earth when I headed into eternity. Perhaps it was their territory the night the coven had reached into the blackness to materialize the dark apparition. But this rough piece of real estate, with its grasses and small hills and trees and fresh, pollutant-free air was mine. It was a piece of heaven that they had turned into hell's terrain.

Now it was time for them to pay.

I peered through the woods and spied two other men walking toward me. They didn't look like they were in a hurry. They probably figured the noise from the dogs came from me. The tall, thin man who had my Glock turned and said something to Scar.

Scar laughed, then spied me. His mouth fell open. "He's got a gun," Scar yelled.

And good aim, I thought. "As Martina sang, 'Roll the stone away, let the guilty pay,' " I said aloud.

Scar tried to aim his weapon, but my shot exploded in his chest and threw him back. He gurgled blood, then hit with a final death splat on the wet ground. His partner fumbled with his gun. He tried to bring it up to his shoulder, but, perhaps because the gun was wet, it slipped from his fingers. By the time he had raised it I had him in my sights. My rifle cracked like thunder. The bullet gave him a third eye in his forehead. His gun dropped by his side. I ran over and grabbed my Glock.

Judas and Jezzy, howling maliciously, dashed off toward the hunting party. I took one look down at the body and grimaced. The dogs had taken most of the man's face and ripped huge, bloody holes in his body.

"Three down. Seven to go," I said.

I didn't expect the coven members to stay and fight. They were not used to prey shooting back. They were not disciplined or trained. I expected them to panic and run, even though they still had a numerical advantage.

The shots had caused the remaining hunters to take cover. They looked at one another and shouted questions.

Geneva flattened behind a stump. A splinter stung my cheek, drawing blood, as her shot blasted the bark on the tree. No, I didn't expect her to cut and run. Others, yes. But not her.

Her husband was behind a rock. He also took aim. His shot whizzed over my head. I fired rapidly, trying to pin them down. I glanced around to ensure no one would get behind me.

Another bullet thunked into the tree. I ran to a higher elevation and dropped down behind a mound. I spied Chubby Hands, the guy with the knife, trying to circle and get behind me. I bounced a bullet off the tree protecting Canterley, then turned toward Chubby. He waited a second, then sprinted toward the next tree. If sprinted is the right word. When the bullet plopped in his side, he yelled as he went down. Blood spurted from the wound. He raised up, one hand over his bleeding side. He was in pistol range now. I used the Glock to put two more bullets in him. He dropped backward and didn't move again.

Yes, I appreciated Pastor Haniford and his intercessors. I didn't doubt they had saved my life. But this was no time to reflect on the Judeo-Christian ethic. This was a time of no mercy and no quarter. A wounded man can still kill you. Chubby would try to kill me as long as he drew breath. Destroy them all, the Lord told the Israelites more than once. Now I know why.

The ground and trees shook as thunder boomed above. Heavier rain broke from the clouds. Perhaps nature was trying to erase the blood. Drops hit the ground, trees, and leaves, giving a rhythm to the carnage.

As Chubby Hands had tried to scramble to my left, Geneva Canterley edged to my right. With a quickness that surprised me, she ran around her husband, then disappeared behind a pine tree. My shot pinged a slide of bark off the pine. Canterley fired in reply. His bullet plunked into the ground about two feet away from me. I put two shots into the tree that protected him. Geneva was on the move again, but as she ran around a rock, her foot slipped on the wet ground. She yelled in surprise, fell, and tumbled down the incline.

I shook my head, shaking off the raindrops from my face. I wiped the rain from my ears, then heard the bloodcurdling screams of agony. Judas and Jezzy had taken another coven member down.

"Let's get out of here," came a voice.

"Stay where you are," yelled Canterley.

"Ten against one. But your demonic god isn't doing too well, is he? How is he going to help you now?" I said.

"We'll see you in hell, Banyon. Just wait."

Two coven members were off to the side. I drew careful aim and lodged two bullets close to them. With the howls of the Dobermans and the pitiful cries of the victim within range of their sight, the two bullets broke them. One man and the black-haired woman turned and fled. They dropped their rifles and ran back toward the lodge.

"Kill them!" Canterley shouted.

The dark Hispanic raised up. He felled the woman first. The male didn't stop for her. But before he took another step, the

Hispanic cut him down. Water and mud flew into the air as he hit the ground. But the Hispanic had exposed himself. I aimed and fired. He jerked violently when the bullet hit him high in the back. He managed to turn around. Blood flowed from below his neck. My bullet had sliced through him.

As the rain drummed on my back I realized I had forgotten Geneva Canterley. I spun around, but my side exploded. Blood and skin splashed on the ground. I rolled over as her next bullet plopped in the mud. She noticed I had dropped the rifle and moved toward me as she fired again. A mistake.

I seized the Glock and brought it up, ignoring the pain in my side. In a second, three dots of red blotted her brown jacket. Without a sound she fell, lifeless, into the mud. I had never shot a woman before, much less killed one. But if I had to start with someone, Geneva Canterley filled the bill. I groaned and stood up.

Then I heard the voice behind me. "Drop your gun."

I slowly turned around. Canterley had scrambled up the hill. He pointed his rifle at me. "You destroyed everything."

Drops of water spotted his face and leaked from his chin. But I didn't think it would affect his aim. Not at this distance.

The orange sun was close to the horizon. The dark orange beams gave the area a funeral atmosphere. It reflected on his face and highlighted the sharp incisors. Judas and Jeezy seemed more human than he did.

"I think the credit for that goes to Ted and Stephanie. I just helped."

"You have no idea how much you will suffer for this, Banyon. Throughout all eternity I will torture you, to pay you back."

I spat on the ground. "I don't think you're going to get your wish. You failed. Your grandiose scheme crumbled. All your people are dead. Your boss isn't going to be happy with you. You won't get your wish in the afterlife."

His growl was as menacing as any the Dobermans had made. "I will get to pay you back. That much will be granted to me." He raised the rifle. "Perhaps I will make you suffer here. One in the gut and I will watch—"

His mouth stayed open, but no sound came out. He looked shocked, if not disappointed. The hole appeared just over his heart. I saw him jerk, then heard the crack of the rifle. I doubted if another shot was needed, but a second hole appeared a micrometer under the first. He gave no sound as he slid onto the wet ground.

I waited for a minute or so until Diego walked into view. He nodded toward me but walked toward Canterley. He crossed himself as he stood over the body. He looked toward me. "It's a terrible thing to kill a man. But he deserved to die."

"They all deserved to die. Every mother's son and daughter of them."

He nodded. "Yes, but it's sad we had to be the ones to kill them."

I held my side and groaned. "It would have been sadder if they had killed us."

A one-note harsh laugh came from Diego. He walked up and looked at the wound. There was both an entrance and exit hole. "I know a man who can help with that, and he doesn't ask any questions."

"Tell me he also has medical training."

"Enough."

"Good. I plan to see Pastor Haniford too. That was a little too close. I don't want to go to the same place Canterley is at."

"Wise decision, amigo."

Before I could move, I heard the sulfurous voice of Geneva Canterley.

"Banyon," she croaked in a deathlike voice that made me feel as if spiders were scurrying over me. Even with three bullets in her, she was alive. Just barely.

She spat out some blood. "You haven't won," she said.

I looked out at the dead bodies of the coven members. "If I haven't won, it sure looks like you lost, lady."

She gritted her teeth against the pain but gazed at me with absolute hatred. "There are others...like us." With her last gasp, she grabbed my shirt. "You are now known in hell. The powers of darkness will take their revenge."

With that, she fell back on the wet ground and went to be with her dark lord.

"If so, you won't be here to see it," I said.

After that, I managed to drive my car three miles to a clearing. Then I climbed into Diego's passenger seat. I didn't want my car at the scene of the carnage. While driving, Diego called 911 and, in his best or worse Spanish, I couldn't tell which, told of hearing shots and seeing bodies and described the site.

Diego's friend was a real professional. I liked the way he cleaned and dressed the wound. Plus, he seemed to have ample antibiotics. I only had sixty dollars cash. He took the money but said not to worry. He was confident I would survive and be around to pay the rest later.

The next day, after taking pain medication, I watched the midday news. An attractive and intelligent brunette told me of the astonishing and horrific discovery by Volusia County deputies. Ten people were found shot and killed at what appeared to be a hunting lodge. After some quick work, two other bodies, long buried, had been discovered. Authorities were noncommittal when asked if they expected other bodies to be found. Both the Florida Department of Law Enforcement and the FBI had been called into the case. The three agencies were puzzled, but some detectives questioned whether the dead individuals had formed some type of murder club.

Nothing was said about the altar in the lodge's basement. I doubted if that information would be released to the public. It was just a bit too bizarre. A day later Diego's friend dropped by and checked my wound. He seemed satisfied that my recovery was going well. I peeled off some twenties and told him I appreciated his expertise.

Pastor Haniford also dropped by to visit me. We had a long discussion. When he left, he was satisfied too. He and his friends had saved my life. I figured I owed them my soul.

Twenty-two

Three days after that I drove into the parking lot of the Volusia County Humane Society and eased between two yellow lines. I wondered if, since I was wounded, I could use the handicap space, but I did not have a blue sticker.

I walked into the building and said hello to the greeters. They knew me. It was not the first time I'd been there. They guided me past the cages and into a private room.

The police had found Judas and Jezzy. They'd had to stun them. Since they had killed at least two humans, they were going to be put down. I didn't want them to die alone. Mark Twain once said, "If you feed a dog and take care of him, he won't turn on you. That's the difference between humans and dogs." There's a lot of truth in that statement.

The veterinarian explained they had already been sedated. I asked how they behaved while in the clinic, and he said very well. Neither Judas nor Jezzy showed any trace of violent behavior.

"Just give me a few minutes," I said.

"Would you like us to bring them in one at a time?"

"No, they can come together. They lived together. They should go out together."

A door opened, and an attendant walked in with the dogs. Jezzy yelped with delight and leaped up, putting her paws on my shoulder. I rubbed behind her ears. She licked my face. I didn't want to sit above them so I eased down on the floor. They sat in front of me, eyes alert, ears attentive. Still, there was a sadness in their faces. Animals know when the end is near.

"I want to tell you two something. Your life was not pleasant. In fact, it was filled with pain and brutality. Even so, you saved my life. So I want to repeat what Pastor Haniford told me." I reached out and stroked both of them. Jezzy moved forward and placed her face on my shoulder.

"A few years ago, one of Pastor Haniford's congregants lost both of her dogs. She'd had them for almost fifteen years and lost both within two months. She was a true animal lover and disconsolate. So, while praying, the Lord showed her a vision of heaven. There were animals there."

I kept petting them while talking. "So the lady asked about the dogs and cats, and the Lord responded, 'These are the animals of the redeemed.' Pastor Haniford believed the story. So I'm claiming you two, and I am redeemed. On your papers, I am now listed as owner, so you're mine. Even if I hadn't cared for my own soul, I would have converted to give you two a shot at heaven. You deserve a good afterlife. It's been a horrid time down here."

The doctor and a nurse came in. They were very efficient.

A minute later, Judas and Jezzy peacefully fell asleep. Jezzy still had her head on my shoulder.

When I left, the doctor mentioned the pet cemetery to me. I asked that they be placed there. I would purchase a monument for each.

Pastor Haniford would come and say prayers for them. Their former owners are in hell, but they would sleep peacefully in hallowed ground.

Stephanie and Ted could sleep peacefully now too. As could Tiffany and Frank.

I will say this for the Canterleys and their demonic friends. They were dedicated. Dedicated to the point of absolute fanaticism.

I hope we have enough people on our side that dedicated. People like Pastor Haniford and his deacons.

Because if we don't....

A WINE RED SILENCE

GEORGE L. DUNCAN

In the balkanized, bizarre,
politically correct world of the future,
sin has not yet been eradicated.
Neither has murder...

Private detective Jerico Drake is used to dealing with a world that has basically rejected goodness. With the nation now balkanized into white, black, and Hispanic sections, and the new breed of "genrich" (genetically sculptured) humans, technology has given evil a few more wrinkles.

Drake's client, the young and lovely Lori Hallendorf, seems like a light in the midst of darkness...even though her life has been marred by tragedy. As Drake investigates her brother's murder, he discovers that he's been targeted by an unrelenting assassin—a robotic killer with a shocking kind of artificial intelligence.

In a world of nanotechnology and genetic engineering, where fantasies are easily fulfilled but dreams turn to ashes, Drake must pursue a deadly trail that will show him both the worst, and the best, of humankind.

Galaxy Gems

George L. Duncan

Think the 21ˢᵗ century is bad?
Just wait until the 23ʳᵈ....

Fighting aliens. Combatting hostile insectoids. Solving cosmic mysteries. Exploring the galaxy. Battling demonic opponents.

It's just another routine day at the office...if you're a Spacehawk, that is.

Love. Honor. Sacrifice. Duty. Blood and Death.

For squadron members Trent Bartley, Tequesta Lynquest, Lupe Martinez, and Sebastian McCloud, it's a great life.

If you survive.

About the Author

GEORGE DUNCAN is a former reporter and now an editorial writer. Although an avid golfer, his game was not nearly good enough to get him on the pro tour, so he became a writer instead. He is the author of three other novels—*A Cold and Distant Memory, A Wine Red Silence,* and *Galaxy Gems,* a collection of sci-fi short stories—and has sold several stories to Christian e-magazines. He is now completing his next novel, *Hoofbeats of the Devil.* Being a mystery fan, Duncan wanted to combine the private detective genre with the supernatural genre, which is what *A Dark Orange Farewell* does.

For more information:
www.sffaithgolfer.com
random bits of information about politics, faith, science, science fiction and, of course, golf
www.oaktara.com

Breinigsville, PA USA
03 February 2010
231903BV00002B/3/P